Michael Wilding's novels and stories include *Living Together, The Short Story Embassy, Wildest Dreams, Wild Amazement, Great Climate*, and the Plant private-eye series, *The Prisoner of Mount Warning, The Magic of It,* and *In the Valley of the Weed*. His documentaries include *Raising Spirits, Making Gold and Swapping Wives: The True Adventures of Dr John Dee and Sir Edward Kelly* and *Wild Bleak Bohemia: Marcus Clarke, Adam Lindsay Gordon and Henry Kendall*. He was born in Worcester, read English at Oxford, and has taught at the University of Birmingham, the University of California at Santa Barbara, and the University of Sydney, where he is emeritus professor.

Cover artist: Benjamin Leader was born in Worcester in 1833 and educated at the Royal Grammar School there and the Royal Academy School.

THE MIDLANDS, AND LEAVING THEM

Other books by Michael Wilding

Fiction

Aspects of the Dying Process
Living Together
The Short Story Embassy
The West Midland Underground
Scenic Drive
The Phallic Forest
Pacific Highway
Reading the Signs
The Man of Slow Feeling: Selected Short Stories
Under Saturn
Great Climate
This is for You
Book of the Reading
Somewhere New: New and Selected Stories
Wildest Dreams
Academia Nuts
Wild Amazement
Superfluous Men
National Treasure
The Prisoner of Mount Warning
The Magic of It
Asian Dawn
In the Valley of the Weed
Little Demon
The Travel Writer

Documentary

The Paraguayan Experiment
Raising Spirits, Making Gold and Swapping Wives: The True Adventures of Dr John Dee and Sir Edward Kelly
Wild Bleak Bohemia: Marcus Clarke, Adam Lindsay Gordon and Henry Kendall

THE MIDLANDS, AND LEAVING THEM

MICHAEL WILDING

Shoestring Press

All rights reserved. No part of this work covered by the copyright herein may be reproduced or used in any means—graphic, electronic, or mechanical, including copying, recording, taping, or information storage and retrieval systems—without written permission of the publisher.

Printed by imprintdigital
Upton Pyne, Exeter
www.digital.imprint.co.uk

Typesetting and cover design by The Book Typesetters
us@thebooktypesetters.com
07422 598 168
www.thebooktypesetters.com

Published by Shoestring Press
19 Devonshire Avenue, Beeston, Nottingham, NG9 1BS
0115 925 1827
www.shoestringpress.co.uk

First published 2021
© Copyright: Michael Wilding
© Cover painting: Benjamin Williams Leader, *In the fields*, 1863, oil on canvas on wood panel, 70.0 × 105.2 cm, National Gallery of Victoria, Melbourne, purchased, 1873 (Photo: National Gallery of Victoria, Melbourne)

The moral right of the author has been asserted.

ISBN 978-1-912524-73-0

Acknowledgements

'The Decline in Importance of the Family' and 'Thank You, Miss' first appeared in *London Magazine*. 'Class Feeling' and 'The West Midland Underground' first appeared in *Stand*. 'Reading the Signs' and 'Gypsies' first appeared in the *New Yorker*.

Other stories first appeared in *Alta, The Bulletin, Casual, Chance International, Man, Newswrite, Outrider, Overland, Southerly, Southern Review, Text,* and *Westerly*.

The stories were originally collected in *The West Midland Underground* (University of Queensland Press), *The Phallic Forest* (Wild & Woolley, and John McIndoe), *Reading the Signs* (Hale & Iremonger), *This is for You* (Angus & Robertson) and *Wild Amazement* (Central Queensland University Press, and Shoestring Press).

The excerpts in 'Coming to an End' are from 'The Tunnel' published in *The Worcesterian* and 'Frrried Potatoes' broadcast on the BBC Morning Story. The excerpt in the second paragraph of 'The West Midland Underground' is from 'A Thousand Languages' by Stephen Wurm in *New Guinea: Prospero's Other Island*, ed. Peter Hastings (Angus & Robertson).

Contents

Reading the Signs	1
Canal Run	5
The Wrath of Farmers	16
Class Feeling	21
Gypsies	31
Jealous of Ali	34
Three Incidents for a Mercia Quartet	40
War and Pacifism	43
On the Road to Stratford	49
The Fir Trees	55
Armistice	63
Nephew's Story	66
Thank You, Miss	72
Don't Go Having Kittens	80
Like Rat Turds to Me	95
The Decline in Importance of the Family	112
The West Midland Underground	134
Coming to an End	144

Reading the Signs

It grew under the apple tree. It got a start because nothing much else ever grew there. We did try potatoes occasionally, but you caught your fork in the tree roots trying to dig them up. So that from the apple tree to the fence at the right was my garden, and from the apple tree to the path at the left was my sister's. She put in rocks and moss and things for the fairies.

It grew there with its stubby wooden stem and its bushy branches of leaves and then this amazing pinkish, purplish bugle of a flower. We let it grow because we had never seen anything like it; even before the flower, it had this presence, this numinosity. But the flower was a clarion of mystery. Then the seed pod formed, green and spiky at first, and then it darkened and became rounded and leathery.

We asked everybody what it was and no one knew. Even Dad must have accepted some of its mystery because he never pulled it up. Even though under the apple tree was not productive and even though he didn't believe in stripping off all unplanted vegetation like some of the people in the avenue, the bigger weeds got pulled up and put on the compost heap.

So nobody knew and we picked the seed pod and kept it in a little fish-paste jar in the kitchen window, sitting in the fish-paste jar like an egg in an egg cup on the windowsill above the sink, among the rubber rings that sealed the fruit we bottled in jars, and the hairpins and the used razor blades and countless other things. Sometimes the robin would hop in through the open window and peck around. Year after year the windowsill was in the robin's territory.

The seed pod cracked open and we kept the dark brown seeds in the bottom of the fish-paste jar through the winter and they stayed on the windowsill with all the other accreted things and got forgotten. The plant died beneath the apple tree and the dried stem was tossed onto a bonfire.

The next year it came again. But the next year it had come all over the rest of England, too. Neighbours had them. The newspapers reported its mysterious appearance throughout the country. The Californian thorn apple, they called it. Jimsonweed. *Datura stramonium*. Said to be deadly poisonous.

'Wonder you didn't poison the lot of us,' Dad said. Poisonous, they all said. No one said it was a hallucinogen. But they stamped them out and burned them just the same.

Once the plant was everywhere and had been named, we didn't know what else to do. We knew there was a mystery but the naming and the reported spread of it were made to do service for the revelation. We never did take any of it, boiled or brewed or powdered or smoked or rubbed into the skin. The newspapers never suggested you could do that. That sort of knowledge hadn't survived. It was about this time that Mum had her fortune read at the village fête and was told that in a few years she'd be doing the same thing herself: reading fortunes. She was always able to read the signs. If she dropped a big knife it would be a tall visitor coming, and a little knife a short visitor. The magpies would fly over the fields, one for sorrow, two for joy. But the uses of the thorn apple had been stamped out in the witch burnings. Everything comes in threes was another of Mum's sayings. But the third year the thorn apple didn't come back. And the seeds had got thrown on the fire because of everyone's saying how poisonous it was. I think that was a mistake, not keeping the seeds.

'That flying saucer you saw,' I asked Mum.

'Oh, Michael, did we?' she says. 'I can't remember now.'

It was like this when I needed my precise time of birth for the astrological chart. 'Here we are. Five. One. Or was that the date? Wait until I find my specs.'

'When we were living up the avenue. You remember.'

The avenue was a row of twenty-seven houses, with fields in front of us – because they hadn't built on the other side of the road – and fields behind. They stopped building when the war started. The prisoners of war used to hoe in the fields at the back.

'We were in the back garden talking one evening and it just came over,' Mum said. 'I can't remember if it was our back garden, even.'

'And it just came over the garden?'

'I think so,' Mum said. 'It wasn't very high. It was just like a bright light. It had a sort of tail, I think.'

'And where did it go?'

'It just vanished. It just went. It wasn't there anymore.'

'No,' said Dad. 'No, no, no, it was in the front of the houses. We were standing in the road. It was going up the river. It was a meteorite. It was going up the river.'

'What, following it along?'

'That's what it looked like.'

Dad wrote to the paper. 'As an iron-moulder, it seemed to me like a glowing red ball of molten iron.'

Sometimes he would be at home with burns on his hands or feet from molten iron that had spilled. Now he is at home dying of emphysema from the foundry dust.

'It was just like molten iron when it comes out of the furnace.'

Mum was furious, embarrassed. She went red.

'I never expected them to print it,' Dad said. 'I just wrote it as information for them.'

Other people in town had sighted it. There were other letters.

'You might have known they'd print it.'

'No, I didn't, so that's that,' Dad said.

Mum was mortified. On the forms at school we wrote 'Engineer' not 'Iron-moulder.' Filling in the forms for university, I went off to a private place and my stomach wrenched for a long time and for 'Father's Profession or Occupation' I crossed out 'Profession' and wrote 'Iron-moulder.'

The man at the appointments board, just before I left, congratulated me. 'Well, well,' he said,' you're tipped for a first, you edited the university paper, you've done very well for an iron-moulder's son.'

Dad said, 'It went along up the river glowing like molten iron and then it exploded. It was a meteorite.'

'There wasn't any noise,' Mum said.

'I didn't say there was any noise,' Dad said. 'It exploded in a big flash.'

'But explosions usually make a noise,' Mum said.

I don't know whether Dad had clipped the letter or not. I've had letters in print that were not intended for print. I think I kept them but kept them beneath dark stacks of things.

'People who've seen them don't seem to talk about them much,' I said.

'That's right,' Mum said. 'We didn't talk about it much, did we?' she said to Dad.

What they talked about was the letter. The shame of being a manual worker and the ridicule for having seen a flying saucer and the breaking of the taboo in revealing these things in print.

Canal Run

I suppose I should be thankful, or pleased, or at least have some feeling of satisfaction, that my school sent me on those social-realist cross-country runs. It provided a group of feelings and sense impressions that I might otherwise have managed to avoid. I'm sure it never meant to; never meant, that is, the social-realist aspect, let alone socialist-realist. The runs themselves it meant. The runs, to me then, were further instruments of taming and torture, cruelties inflicted to show up my inabilities, inabilities I affected to despise until I did come to despise them, consider them not inabilities at all but evidence of my separateness from the bulk of people, the unpleasant mass, from the bulk of boys I disliked and the attitudes I hated.

I never remember adjusting to the school, but adjust gradually I did so that the teaching of the school, the conformities it demanded, the attitudes it bred, gradually I came to accept. They became my attitudes. The fuss of giving up one's seat in the bus to old ladies and old gentlemen; it was a commendable discipline, and now still I find it a stock reaction; but the reasons for the discipline were not the reasons that now prompt me to, occasionally, surrender a seat. Now I do it from sympathy, say. But then it was a matter of going to a better school, of being polite, of being conscious of our separateness, of our distance from the lack of polish and courtesy of the secondary-moderns; we had to wear our caps, and straight, and eating in the street was punishable by a Saturday morning detention. We were trained to be gentlemen. We were often lectured at the end of prayers about dress; the headmaster had seen some pupil wearing jeans at the weekend; this wasn't good enough. Certain haircuts were forbidden. School blazers were not to be worn with any other clothes than official school uniform; in the holidays, walking along a Devon beach or climbing some sheep-smoothed mountain in Wales, I wore my khaki drill shorts and open-neck aertex shirt with my blazer; and felt guilt. I dreaded a normal afternoon school detention; a Saturday morning was ignominy. I accepted these rules with annoyance. I accepted them. The A stream always accepted then, otherwise you went into a B or C stream class. There the undesirable dominated. Their ties were striped school ties, but somehow more boot-lacey; their collars were more cut-away, their shoes were slip-ons, their socks were coloured. But in the A stream I dressed conventionally; I parted my hair conventionally when I parted it; I became like everyone else in the A stream. When in German conversation I was asked what job my father did, I blushed furiously. In the A stream everybody's father was vaguely white collar. I was never any good at French or German. In English though you could lose your identity in the person of someone else in the book. I was good at that. I had already submerged my personality in the A stream. I liked English. Later I studied Fowler's *Modern English Usage* and made my speech more precise. I excised the extremes of Midlands accent. I said bus instead of buzz, and why? instead of woi? And I never called the canal the cut.

I hated the canal. I hated the canal because I hated runs, and because of the associations of some of those runs. And I hated runs because I was no good at sport. I think now I could have been better at runs. Better, never good. But then, I hated them. I don't regret it. It was hating runs that first made me hate other things; that, and being hated for hating them. Games were the first thing I stuck at; first and almost immediate. They made the first crack in the neo-Gothic facade of the school hall, the first rip on the neat navy blazer, the first gag or stain on the regulation grey shirt. It had been model before. Its cheeks had been rosy to blushed red; its avoidance of detention exemplary; its interest in what we called filth typical, its language good; its academic standard a perfect, desirable average. No irregularity. But games were bad, and so House Spirit became ultimately, as the last report said, non-existent. And into that niche of decay the other germs were able to penetrate.

I hated the canal because I hated running. And because I hated running I hated other things. And by hating those other things that running to some degree symbolized and supported, I came to adopt a positive attitude, and by return came, though not to love, at least not to hate, the canal. I could view it as a creation of some social, even scenic interest. Everything that when I had had to run along it I hated for the filth and squalor, for the immediacy, now distanced I can see more objectively. And some of those prejudices I held against the canal I no longer hold, because of that canal's influence.

It was grey. Sometimes, I suppose, the sun must have shone. It cannot always have been monochrome and damp, sad and blot grey like the screen of a newspaper photograph. Of course there were colours – the long corrugated iron fence of the city football ground was painted a green, a vivid unnatural green, and the bricks of the many bridges were a chipped and carved red, and the running shorts were navy-blue or white, spattered with the red-brown clay from the marl banks. And yet, though thinking back I can see underneath the red arch the green fence with the white or blue figures running, slouching or scuffling, puddle-splashing beside it, it is still all grey. Because the colours were not alive. To me they were cold and hand-chapped and nose-runny; and hateful. And when I hated I closed up my spirit; I did not hate with a fiery red intensity, an upsurge of poster paint flung against a wall, nor with a black violent fury, a thuggery and brutality of obliteration. But when I hated I screwed up my soul and screwed up my eyes and screwed up my body so that I stood there, bent at the waist, my arms and legs half bowing over, half turned at the waist away to one side, away and down, the reverse of a sculptured discus thrower. White there, against the corrugated iron, and screwed up like that, the self had enough to do just to breathe, so cramped, there was no room to see colour, no room to observe, no room to be furious or angry; but a dead, withdrawing hatred, like the wasteland from which God has withdrawn his presence; in my solipsistic world, I was the god, and withdrawing my presence I withdrew all the light and life from it; and there was nothing but a greyness and dullness, a hatred and defeat, a dulled hatred that did not hate enough and do other than run to the end of the course and back again, hand in my name to whoever was waiting to check names, and run or walk back, in the grey twilight. It was grey, too, because we only ran in the spring term – spring, a sad misnomer for the three winter months of the new year. In the summer there was the sun; but not in the spring; there was nothing to detract from the greyness.

And the stillness. The cold, grey water never moved. It was ruffled by the occasional blast of wind, but it never flowed. At the locks, a clear trickle fell through the rotten timbers – but it fell to a still, stagnant pond covered with a slime of dust and oil, floating milk bottles and stalks of grass. The collections of flotsam were always neat. The components clung together with a natural adhesion and formed a smooth edge, a smooth curved edge, which bordered them smooth and still. The dust and debris were collected inside, so from the towpath it looked like an aerial photograph of floating logs near a Canadian saw mill. But I had no eyes for its beauty then. It was too near.

It was unnatural, banked up in places above the level of the surrounding land, man-made, narrow, grey, like death. People often drowned in it, though not as often as my imagination made out. Rushes grew in clusters in certain parts. I never remember seeing bull-rushes, nothing as interesting, nothing as natural as that. But the dead, dried reeds stuck there, rising from the grey slime through the sick water into the frosted or drizzling air. There were so few boats now that the reeds grew easily; not right across – there was traffic enough to stop that – but in wide strips along one bank or the other, never both; the boats didn't need a wide channel, they were only as wide as the constricted locks, and if they kept to the one side the reeds took over the other. We hardly ever saw one of the boats. In the summer, perhaps, from the cricket field, we'd see the top of one slowly pass, obscured by fences and hedges from our sight; but in the winter even the boats seemed to curl in on themselves and shrink down into the depths of the earth; and on the surface only dead stalks, brittle grit, cloying red mud that dried on your pumps to a colourless dried sickness, dried reeds, and the thin water like the blood of a dead monster, a sick monster – thin and grey and poisonous, oozing out of its slaughtered body and spreading for miles and miles.

The towpath was of grit, asphalt or slag, some by-product of some industry that had started when the canals were being cut, an industry as unpleasant and death-aligned as the dead canal, an industry somewhere north in the Black Country to which the canal ran, where the terrace of stark coffin houses that backed onto the canal was multiplied into an infinitude of identical terraces backing onto each other, each with the same grey roof and cheap, worn red bricks, each cramped and sunless as the other, with a slit in the brickwork to serve as an entrance, a crevice through which each insect worker crept home to his cell at the same time in the grey evening as every other insect worker, and crept out again in the grey morning at the same time as every other insect worker, and left his wife to clean or neglect the coffin as she would, while he toiled – romantic words for the unromantic wilderness – and trade boomed and canals were replaced by railways and prosperity increased and increased and everyone thrived and a hundred years later as we ran or slouched or scuffled along the towpath people still lived in the coffins at the end of those grey soiled strips of garden that reached onto the railings along the path. And the people who lived in them still hadn't prospered much, and they viewed us with a hostility because we were the grammar school, and though it was post-'44, a grammar school was still a grammar school, and their children sometimes, as we ran back at the end of the run, and the other schools had finished for the day and the children were at home playing on the canal bank or in the streets that led from the school's back gate to the towpath, the children playing there would call out 'Ragged Gutter Sweepers' or 'Rotten Gutter Snipes', after the initials of the Royal Grammar School; because tradition dies hard, and while they lived in the houses of the industrial tradition they retained the attitudes of the industrial tradition. And looking back now I can see no reason for their ever having done otherwise; but to me, then, to someone who had been cut off from every tradition, and the graft to a fresh one was still uncertain and painful – though no one suspected that it might not take – to me then it was hurtful and one more reason for the screwing up of myself and hating the runs and the canal.

The grit of the towpath was edged against the water by blue bricks, making a border all the way along this part of the waterway – though perhaps not in the country, the country the canal did pass through, though for us it was a thing of the town. The blue bricks I hated. My grandparents, both families of my grandparents, lived in Victorian houses where there were blue bricks. Blue bricks for me then meant decrepitude and old age and the solid uninspiredness of dark Victorian houses; blue bricks and those terraced houses backing onto the canal, houses whose gardens were fenced by an iron railing, a railing of iron spiked stakes, held at top and bottom by an iron horizontal strip. This blackened once pitched now corroded dead iron, standing there not threatening particularly, not doing anything particularly, but existing in its gaunt corroded blackness, that iron and the blue bricks and the washing in the back gardens, sordid washing of slips and petticoats and bloomers and long woollen pants, washing that offended my twisted, retracted spirit with its prudishness and Puritanism of repressed sex that we all held, and that offended an aesthetic sense as then undeveloped, that iron was the dead staked file of bones that lined that lifeless run. And that aesthetic sense was hurt by the shoddiness of the terraces and the blue edging bricks, the dull lumpishness of it all, an industrialism untempered by any thought of design; but how much was that aesthetic sense also moulded by the surroundings, how much did the twisted grey hatred of running become rationalized into aesthetic principles, or become enmeshed with other revulsions of sex and C streams and secondary-modern homes? Now I can see the canal as an engineering achievement, and find pleasure in the industrialism of its nature; yet, perhaps, even this is an aesthetic slumming; and the early dislike, now, perhaps, repressed, may still exist, or be turned on its head in a stubborn reversal, the hated loved and the loved despised.

Dog-shit and dandelions and clumps of grass bordered the towpath – a towpath that no longer was trodden by horses; and the dandelion leaves and flowers were poor and stunted and bruised, even lacerated by the grit; and the grass was withered and dried as it broke through the grey-blue ash or the cracks where the mortar had crumbled from between the blue bricks. And occasionally a tussock of grass would be floating on the dead surface of the canal, and in its green incongruity it would be an offence, thrown there by some gardener from one of the grey-soiled gardens – gardens whose soil, grey from tipping ashes on, and from the soot-laden winter fogs and factory smoke, could grow little but stunted peas and ramshackle lean-tos – or by some boy who wanted to throw something other than bits of wood or the asphalt that would only sink to the mud at the bottom.

Past the row of terraces, past the hideous green-painted iron surrounding the football ground – I never remember having been there – the path eventually came to one of the small worn bridges and we crossed to the other side; it was no better, but less oppressive. Here the houses were ended; the track was still gritted and the canal was still dead, but the houses were ended, and we left the towpath for an open scrubland of grass and clay.

It was still running and I hated running. It was still slipping in puddles or trying to jump over them, but the grit was now replaced by marl. That deep red clay was even more treacherous, its surface impossible to grip with the worn rubber soles of gym pumps, so that at times, when we left the towpath and began to scramble up the sides of the banks of marl, I had to go down on all fours, and my hands would be cold and sore and covered with the red sticky mud. Marl doesn't seem a country feature to me. Oh yes, it was in the open. The oppression of the houses and the grit path was past. We were running over the oozing red mud between the canal and more of the grim terraced houses. This was a brief escape from the rainy dullness of the town, a track over the waste, a short cut from one bunch of terraces to the canal bridge and over that to another clutter. Houses were on both sides; this was an oasis. There was a lack of constriction. The wind blew across even chillier. It was higher. The track wound up the side of the ridge of clay knolls; but they weren't country hills, they weren't at all rustic. They were being cut away. I doubt if they exist now. They were being carved from the one side, like a half-eaten blancmange. Excavators and bulldozers sliced away the sticky red clay, and lorries carried it to the brickworks, the brickworks whose chimney you could see for miles, the brickworks that made the cheap coarse red bricks for the cheap coarse houses, and smoked out from its cheap red brick chimney to soot over the gardens of those houses, to choke the breathing of the people who lived in those houses, to soil the washing hung on lines stretching down the ash-soiled gardens, to grime over the window panes and cheap red bricks. It wasn't the country we ran through, but the industrial wasteland, the undeveloped heath land that exists round railway stations or disused coalfields; the image of that Black Country in the north. It could be used for factory sites when there was the incentive to build a new factory, or for rubbish dumps to burn the refuse the corporation dust carts collected, or for free tips to leave worn out old cars, their useful parts torn from them and the skeleton left there to rust among the tin cans and scrubby bushes, or for the youth of the city, the teenage workers of the factories who lived in the terraces of the rehoused council estates not far away, to copulate on. Scrubland that was dark at night. Contraceptives floated on the canal surface, or rolled down the vertical sliced side of the marl banks and amused the excavator drivers the next day, and perhaps mixed with clay in some uniform brick. I would have disapproved of that then. Thinking back it is hard to see exactly when one's consciousness of sex began and became a desire for, a whole youth's looking for, fulfilment. Then, though, there was only a strong sense of sin and shame and dirt; no lyricism, and none of the hatred. It was wrong and furtive and C stream; which was another way of saying lower class.

The track I forget in all its details now. It wound places. It passed more houses. It came to a main road where we ran on the black tarmac pavements and women shopping noticed us and took no notice. And sometimes I would be embarrassed and nervous and unwilling to be noticed and wanting to be anywhere but there and hating the conspicuousness of it all. And other times I would be the martyr and love it all, the position of importance that I gave myself and that none of the pram-pushers and pensioners was at all aware of. And then off the main road again. It was here that it happened. The secondary-modern school was here. It had two departments. Boys and girls. There was no liaison between either department. Only after hours. They were brother and sister schools. They were built on part of the wasteland, which from the girls' school stretched on down to the canal. I must have been about twelve.

Running occasionally, walking most of the time in feeble self-destroying rebellion, I was in the last, useless group of the straggling line of runners. Along the canal we had come, along the track and over the slippery marl and then briefly through the streets till back we turned to the marl, to the soft, slippery track that passed the school and plunged down towards the canal again. It was mid-afternoon. Sometimes our runs were after school, sometimes in the afternoon; I forget the distinction. The girls were having their playtime, and the playground lined part of the track, fenced off by wire netting. Inside they played on the concrete yard. Some were standing by the netting and looking through at us running past. I don't know how old they were, but presumably about our age, about eleven or twelve or thirteen.

The track started to descend, started down the gradient to the bridge, a path of stones and marl winding through the dried grass of the scrubland. As I got over the crest and started following it down, past the girls' playground, I could see the runners in front of me, slithering down towards the bridge. But before them, a few yards in front of me, on a tussocky stretch of grass rising up from the track, a group of boys was standing. Not many of them. They weren't in my form; C stream. Two or three were lying down on their backs. Tired, I thought, or with the stitch. I looked as I moved past in my half walk, half trot. The girls, too, were looking, from the other side of the wire netting. But the boys weren't, at least not primarily, recovering from the stitch. Some were giggling a bit. The two or three lying on their backs were pissing into the air, firing a jet of piddle high upwards, that bowed over in a parabola. The girls on the other side of the netting were giggling as well. They were interested; it was something they couldn't do, I think I knew that then. I went past, along the track that twisted down to the bridge, and before it bent round the contour of the bank and out of sight of this, I looked back. The image froze, of the blue-shorted white-shirted group, one sitting up, some standing, two or three lying on their backs, one at least still pissing; and behind the netting the girls, and the scrub bank falling down to the still, cold canal. Particularly I remembered the face of the one boy, the one whose idea it obviously was, the one who was obviously the suggester of evil. It was a smiling face. But when in the bathroom mirror I looked at home at my reflection with no trace of a smile, it was the same. It was the same, his face was my face, we might have been brothers. Nobody before had ever remarked on it, remarked that that person in the C stream whose name even I didn't know, looked like me. Why hadn't they? Or hadn't they noticed? I dared ask no one in case for the first time they noticed that resemblance by my drawing their attention to it. If I kept quiet, perhaps no one would ever see the likeness. I prayed, I think, at night. I think I prayed; prayed that I might change my appearance and not look like him, I did not pray that he might change, I prayed that I might, because my face that was like his face was a reflection of evil, and I wanted to lose a face that showed up the wrong and dirtiness clearly to whoever looked. It was torment to see him at school; but worse was the uncertainty, worse was the lack of knowing, was I the same as he was? I hadn't lain there in the grass, pissing in the air, my prick stiff and throbbing. But might I? Might I in future act as he had acted? Were the seeds of that, were the dirtiness and evil lying inside me, waiting? So that one day in the future, I would do that? I didn't want to. But I knew things could change, that the me now would not be the me of the future; I knew that that would happen in any case; but I didn't want the me of the future to be like that likeness of me; if I was to change, it was not, oh God, to be a change to that corruption. For months afterwards when I got home midday and night, I ran upstairs to the bathroom and looked at my face in the mirror.

The Wrath of Farmers

Returning to my home town again in my mind, preparatory to returning in my body, I find not unpredictably or indeed unexpectedly that I hold off. Is it that having explored it already, thought about it so much when I lived there and knew nowhere else, I have written all I would ever want to write, having recalled all I would ever want to record? Or is it that there are unrecorded but not unrecallable episodes, things I should yet look into? The old familiar tautening of the stomach muscles. But the stabs and jabs of pain, are they just the splinters from scraping the barrel and a sign it's time to move on, but I have moved on, now I've moved back? Or are these the jabs of pain and tenderness of the as yet unrecorded episodes of trauma and angst and ill-repressed horror? Of course I could return looking for happy stories, comic stories, and then it would just be the pain of laughing.

Mushrooms were our last link with Germanic communality. The shared landholdings had gone, the common lands had been enclosed, now we had no land. But my father still persisted in some of the old ways. We still collected firewood, blackberries, horse manure. The horse manure mixed with water and turned into liquid manure fed the garden that produced pretty well all our vegetables. But some things were still untamed, shy, elusive. You had to look for mushrooms, they were not something you could cultivate. There were fields where mushrooms could be expected to be found year after year, and then one year there wouldn't be any, or one year the field would have been ploughed and the pasture burned. Then sometimes they would appear in a new field, or a field returned to pasture after years of having been ploughed, and with horses grazing it it would produce mushrooms. Whenever you found them you picked them, great big field mushrooms the size of dinner plates, that was the phrase that was always used. Of course when they were fried they shrank down in size. Fried with bacon for breakfast. They were best found early morning and when my father discovered them growing in a field only a field away from where we lived, he would get up early on a weekend morning to pick them. I can't remember now whether it was a Saturday or a Sunday morning. The old lady who gathered sticks on a Sunday went up into the moon, my Aunt told me, sitting in front of the fire I'd been gathering sticks for that day, Sunday, just this year. How could I ever have forgotten? But I'd managed to. By living in a country where you don't have fires. Don't have fireplaces. Wouldn't mind a fire in winter once in a while.

The early morning meadows at the edge of town, the sun on them like the folds of a warm, soft, glowing blanket, transparent and sucking up the morning dew. Amidst the cowpats and horsepats the fresh surprised mushrooms. We only ever ate field mushrooms, the rest were held to be poisonous, and many were.

There was a farmer's house overlooking the field, an urban-looking raw, red brick, two storey villa with blank red walls like a fortress, like the end of a terrace. This year it is empty, boarded up, uninhabitable because it has no mains water, sewer, or power. Next year no doubt it will be renovated. But at this time of the mushrooms they lived there, the farmer and his wife, with pump water, a wood-burning range, and oil lamps. They would have lived by the seasons, by the light. Every day, even Sundays, he would be up in those beautiful fresh fragrant mornings, shaving at the window, looking across his fields.

'No, no,' said Dad. 'I would never have gone on a Sunday morning. That was the terrible thing, you see,' he said, chuckling.

He'd walked home from church with a friend who was a sidesman. Sidesmen handed out and collected the prayer books and hymn books when you went in and out of church and took the collection, passing the big wooden plate with the green felt base so that the money put in didn't jingle, passing the plate from row to row down the church, standing at the end of each row of pews watching its progress, policing it no doubt so that nobody palmed a few coins back into their hand instead of giving, could there have been such dark suspicions? I'm sure there could. The friend was lamenting the good old days when you could find field mushrooms, and my father told him where there were some growing.

'I never expected he would go on a Sunday,' Dad said. 'Fancy that, a sidesman.'

He'd taken a bag and he'd half filled it when there was an awful confrontation. An enraged farmer, with a shot gun, berating him.

'And I've seen you here every weekend.'

'No you haven't, I've never come before.'

'I've seen you. Don't you bloody tell me no lies. I'll call the bloody police. And if you try to move I'll bloody shoot you too. Every bloody weekend I've seen you. And a bloody Sunday too. Wait till I seen the vicar. I've been waiting for you. I knew as I'd catch you eventually. Never expected to catch a sidesman, though. Wait till I seen the vicar.'

Not that there was much likelihood of that. He was one of the heathen, I think, that farmer. There was a lot of heath country, houses scattered their distance from each other, not clustered together round a church.

'Though,' Dad said, 'you can see why people stay heathens when they see the way respectable churchgoing sidesmen behave.'

Later Dad got baptized and confirmed and became a sidesman himself. And we'd pretty well stopped going for mushrooms by then. It was getting too risky. Once you've encountered the wrath of a farmer you're pretty heavily traumatized. This was only wrath encountered by proxy. But when you've encountered the authentic, even the tale of the proxy resonates.

Across the road from where we lived were fields where cabbages and peas and potatoes were grown. Occasionally we would have to go in there to retrieve a ball we'd thrown or kicked over the railings. But generally we kept out. There was little enough enticing, anyway. Once, however, we investigated some glass cloches. We were examining what was in them when there was a shout from down the hill where the field sloped into the withies along a stream. It was like a scarecrow come to life, the featureless old flapping jacket and floppy hat gesticulating and calling out and, we soon realised, coming towards us. We ran. The shout of a farmer is an ugly shout. The sort to turn your bowels to water. That is its intent. Not even a farmer enraged. Just a farmer, a regular, typical farmer's shout has enough rage, they are in perpetual rage against the public and the city and government and nature and small boys. Maybe the chemical companies keep them sedated now, maybe the superphosphates and the weed-killers and insecticides gently narcotize them. I don't know. I've kept well away from farmers since this moment of terror as we heard the bloodcurdling 'Oi', the Bacchic 'io' of rejoicing reversed into this trumpeting of trouble, and saw him pounding up the slope between the rows of peas, and we dropped the cloches and ran, ran out of the field, over the railings, down the road past half a dozen houses, up the gap between the houses to the field at the back, and then my partner in crime went his way right and I went my way left, past the backs of the houses, then over the back fence, down the garden path, through the back door and up the stairs into my bedroom and a quickly locked door. And the farmer pounding after me, past the astonished neighbours gardening in the mid-morning weekend, past the scents of fresh peas and freshly chopped mint sauce wafting along the garden path, over the back fence, our back fence, and down to where Dad stood.

'Had me worried,' said Dad. 'I thought he was going to have a heart attack. Shouldn't be running around like that at his age.'

And upstairs, panting on the bed, I lay like all those movie protagonists I was yet to see who've climbed a staircase only to find a grille at the top. I just hoped they didn't let him in. I was horrified that he'd followed me into the garden. I thought I might have given him the slip. Or the fence might have restrained him. A social taboo. For all the fuss farmers make of fences, it's amazing how little respect they show for anybody else's.

I can't remember whether I might have had a few pea shells in my pocket, fresh young peas eaten from the pod being very succulent. I guess I could have. Nor can I remember how Dad saved me, but saved I was. No one dragged me out of the bedroom that I can recall. This is probably one of those incidents I don't want to remember. What I do remember are the important things, like keep well away from farmers, and make sure there are no farmers around when you go into a field, always look to see whether they mightn't be bent double and out of your line of vision, or wielding their cut-throat razor in the bathroom window overlooking the field you're in.

Class Feeling

I've been intending to write you a story for a long time, now, D. And it's taken a long time because I've wondered what story to write, what sort of story to write before deciding on something, some event or imagining, that would seem the thing I wanted. And so I've thought in categories, I've thought of the impression I wanted to make on you, the sort of reaction I wanted you to have. At first I wondered; when first you mentioned it, asked me to write a story, I decided it was probably just another social move, something said at one of those parties I perhaps met you at, or to which you perhaps invited me, standing amongst people who went to so many of those parties and knew all their friends who went to them, with them, me uneasy and trying not to let you see that except for you I knew no one and wanted to talk to no one, and endeavouring – whether it was sherry or champagne or beer – to get drunk as quickly as possible so I could either pick up some girl I afterwards wouldn't like (and I rarely picked up anyone) or more often so I could just get drunk; and you looking (and this isn't the place for compliments that anyway I was too diffident to give then either) so obviously assured in it all; and if you weren't, you did look it; to ask over a drink that I should write a story for you, for you, could so easily have been just pleasantness, the sort of soothing or taming I rather expected, making that one thing I'd happened to tell you (and it was only telling; you betrayed no confiding) into something on a par with the sherry your friends offered me. That was the way I looked at it, and I suppose it shows how little we understood each other. But when you asked again – and that time you were so diffident about it, you were asking as if you really felt it was asking for something, as if I had to put myself out for it, asking again because you thought I'd said Yes and then not bothered, or forgotten, and I hadn't forgotten – that time I intended to write a story for you. And, as I say, I've been intending a long time, thinking over the possibilities. Because just any story wouldn't do, and the stories I had been writing were written not with you, or indeed with anyone, in mind; so to send you just a story would miss the important thing, the having written it for you, and the relationship between the story and you; because unless there was some relationship, well, the *for* you would be meaningless. And the possibilities always came into one group, and that was of writing something that would shock you. And some of the nastier incidents that had happened to me, or that had been recounted to me about people I knew and so could visualise and recreate – as imagining is not something I can do without a germ for the story – I turned over as possibilities. And not only the particularly nasty, but those that would show some way of life alien to yours – and alien with all its positive connotations, and not just different. But I think you wouldn't have been terribly shocked; certainly not surprised, because you knew all about that, all those attitudes in me, anyway; you would know particularly that necessity to shock, to assert the unpleasant, to be – I noticed it – cruel. And so the pick-ups of barmaids or the midnight drunkenness on motorways, the criminal fringe and Bohemian fornications of the provinces, I don't think they would have been very shocking; and I think to have told them in this way would have been to have missed their significance, spoilt their images.

This attitude towards you may sound infantile or rude but I'm not telling you to make apology. I'm trying merely to be nearly honest, and to tell you the story I've decided to tell you, I need to be honest, and perhaps need to avoid getting diverted into apologies. But I don't think you should be surprised at this; this need to shock you saw in my hostility when I used to talk to you – I loved to come and talk to you but there was always that hostility, covering inefficiently I suppose a shyness; and it came from the old business of different backgrounds, different childhoods, different, I think, futures. And all this business of barmaid and waitress heroines in the suggestive half-light of our provincial wide-boy pubs is to show you this different life – this life that even so isn't really my life; but I can pretend it is and push it forward as a punch in the face of the bourgeoisie, especially your cultured and literate metropolitan bourgeoisie. Because whatever they were, those heroines weren't cultured or literate. But, as I say, this sort of thing, though clearly not your background, isn't mine either, and I can't deceive either of us by those corner-of-the-mouth utterances. I retain them, though, even though I'm out of that boring and hopeless world. Exactly which one I'm in now I don't know – except that it's not yours; that I always refused to enter – and honestly I don't think there was ever any possibility; because if I had, and hadn't hated it, it would have been only through my having become something other than I was, by abandoning all the things that assure me I was and am anything. But back to the bar, identifying myself as that sort of culture hero is dishonest. And if the purpose of writing a story for you that was unpleasant arose from this background business, the most honest thing to do would be to write a story about this different background, to show some of the differences actually being lived, to show them as they really were, in the usual phrase. This, after all, is where the hostility originates. And this does seem the best thing, to write about a time when you didn't know me, probably didn't conceive of the possibility of such existences – sorry, but that reaction persists – about a time when our lives were very different. Perhaps, so geographically far away now I don't feel the need to shock you any more – getting older or communicating only, and irregularly, by airmail; or again maybe the conditions of life in this democratic country – and though we use the phrase ironically we know it refers to a real quality – remove the pressures I used to feel. Or maybe, this story will be far more shocking than any I could deliberately have planned; that's perhaps why I've never properly told it to anyone; and writing it, I think I shall be able to tell it to you; but I'm sure, sitting there with each other, on those depressed Sunday afternoons, I could never have told it.

I'm thinking of the time when I must have been twelve or thirteen. I don't really know where you were then, whether at your prep school, if girls have prep schools, or at your ladies' college; so not knowing, I won't try to point comparisons. I anyway was at the Royal Grammar School. The Royal was important and the headmaster used to be very annoyed and even childish when people addressed letters to the Boys' Grammar School. And this is a point of some significance. Because Royal, you see, mattered; though when I used to stand across the road from the school, waiting for the bus home, I never noticed the statue of Queen Elizabeth who gave us our regality, a stone carving in a niche high in the old red brick neo-Gothic hall. But she was there, presiding over the traffic, her back to the school. And even though I was unaware of her effigy, the tone her regality set I certainly couldn't avoid; and certainly never considered avoiding. Putting on my cap and blazer I put on a new set of behaviour. I suppose schools are pretty much the same everywhere in encouraging attitudes, and I suppose there's always likely to be some clash. Later I read sensitive memoirs of schooldays, and appreciated that. For me at this age, though, there was hardly a clash, instead a totally new set of attitudes, forgetting, even, that there ever had been any other.

In being told not to eat in the street and to give up one's seat on the bus to ladies, in having frequent diatribes about touching one's cap to the staff one met in the street, in all this there was borne along an attitude – a whole habit of mind that caused such pronouncements and which filtered into our consciousnesses through the sediment of the specific instructions. And strangely there were no rebels; there were no rebels in the A stream. The type of person who entered the A stream came from the type of background that conformed, and that anyway shared those attitudes. And yet, had I been aware of the complexity of that existence around me, had I been aware of other things in not only life but even in that school, I would have realised that the frequent diatribes about touching one's cap, the addresses after prayers about not wearing school blazers with non-regulation trousers after school hours, arose from some continual disregard of the authority and attitudes. But I guess that even if I'd thought about this – and the point is I could never have thought about this – I would have drawn myself aside from these sins and transgressions of the C stream.

I'm drawing out, you see, D., an elaborate and too long defence. I didn't intent this, I didn't intend a defence at all; when I first began to remember this story I intended to be conscious of the indefensible wrong. Yet I don't want to say that, because I don't like to make final, facile judgements on my own past, because there is no one to give the defence. But I don't want to become defensive, as that would lose the point of telling the story. And if I could just begin to tell the story, all this would be unnecessary, surely, as you would be able to make your own decision.

I used to catch the bus home from the stop opposite the school from where, if I had looked across the road from the stop to the school itself, I could have seen that statue of Queen Elizabeth. But I never remember noticing it. There was a traffic island in the middle of the road which we had to use and this meant coming out of the main gate, walking ten yards down the pavement to cross by the island, and then walking ten yards back to the bus stop which was opposite the gates. I always used the island, despite the inconvenience; none of us dared not to. Though thinking back I can see the faces of some people who ran straight across from the gate to the bus stop; they were all in C streams. I remember once that my bus was pulling into the stop as I came out of the gate. So I ran those ten yards to the crossing desperately; and a prefect shouted at me to stop running. So I stopped, and missed the bus. Those were the sort of rules we had, those the prefects.

I used to wait then at this bus stop, standing by a cast iron lamp-post on the pavement's edge, or leaning against the stone window-sill of the public house there, or sometimes looking in the window of the shop that sold bicycles and toys, that was next door to the pub. This afternoon I was late going home. Normally I had left at four and caught the bus at once, so that by the time my father arrived home from work I had had my tea. This day, though, I was later. Possibly I had been involved in some house games or something, something that I was so clearly no good at and something that had possibly annoyed me and shown up my lack of accepted and normal abilities, so that I was feeling strongly those pressures and my lack of living up to them.

It was late and I wanted to go home and read and I was turning over my irritations in my mind when I saw my father cycling home from town, saw a shape, anyway, just past the next bus stop, the bus stop nearer to town, that looked very much as he looked.

My father was an iron-moulder. You probably don't know what that is; they never did at school, they always confused it with ironmonger. There were always forms asking for parents' occupation or profession. I remember my mother – I think this must have been when I first went to the school – wanted to put engineer; I'm sure she did put it, and I know in French conversation classes I always said engineer, which was so wide a category. It wasn't until right at the end of the sixth form that I ever discovered the father of one of my friends was a taxi-driver, or even admitted to my father's being what he was, found out that not every parent was, to use a term I always thought innocuous but which maddens my father, white collar; but we all acted as if ours were.

My father most certainly was not white collar. And seeing him cycling towards me in his old trilby hat, his grimy mackintosh with a canvas haversack hung across it, with dark serge or ex-air force or ex-postman's trousers, clipped in at the ankles above his boots, so that they ballooned out around his calves, and all of these, his working clothes, covered in the black sand and soot he worked in, and the trousers holed with burns from flying sparks or molten metal, seeing him cycling towards me like this I wanted not to have to acknowledge him. It seemed to me unfair that such was my father.

I remember this in static shots; first of my father – or what seemed to be my father in the distance. And to have to meet him outside the school was terrible; and next I remember that standing at the bus stop was a prefect – I can remember his name and face but those would be irrelevant for you as you wouldn't know what associations these had; the important thing is that he was a prefect, leaning against the lamp-post waiting for his country bus; and then I remember the next shot of my father's form approaching, becoming gradually firmer, stronger.

You probably, I said, don't know what an iron-moulder is. I know that I don't. I don't want to have to involve anyone else in this, but my mother did I think discourage any inquisitiveness about what an iron-moulder was, discourage it simply and passively by not inquiring herself. It was a dirty and sweaty job, so my father's working clothes were hung in the garage – he changed in the back kitchen and washed himself there, except on Friday nights when he had a bath – and they were brought back into the house when he went to bed – and we as children were already in bed – and put by the fireplace to air and to dry out the sweat, ready for him to put on again in the living room in the early morning, while we were still in bed. His hat, that dirty trilby, and Mac, of course, never came into the house. Nor did his great hard boots. It was the sort of job that made his clothes smell and keeping them outside kept the smell outside and in the house we never asked questions about his work. We heard about his frustrations and quarrels, his disputes with the bosses and his being underpriced for a job, as sitting in his working clothes he drank cups of tea before beginning tiredly the labour of washing. But exactly what iron-moulding was I never knew. My mother hated it. He would always find this irrational, as anyway he washed his own shirts, so the dirt didn't affect her. But she would say his washing each night in the kitchen made such a mess; or that it left him so tired. She hated his cycling home through town and up the avenue dressed as he worked. He worked in a blue rough shirt – you know the sort, some of the theatre people used to wear them at Oxford – and on top of this an old torn waistcoat. He got through several waistcoats but I remember at the moment one belonging to a suit he had had – the suit, I think, he got married in, blue with a thin white stripe of thread in it. But coming home he would have on top of this a worn old jacket, any jacket that had got too disreputable for the garden, or maybe one mum had picked up at a church rummage sale she was helping at; and on top of the jacket the Mac; and a colourless scarf around his neck. And this mass of clothing he would slowly cycle in – he didn't want to catch a chill after the heat of the foundry's furnaces. There was a degree of cussedness in him which explains his coming home like that, and he must have come home like that the nearly fifty years he worked at that job, starting it at thirteen; a degree of cussedness because he could have changed at work; there were – after maybe thirty years of working at that job – showers installed. He could have washed and changed. But he wouldn't. So he came home in this way. Sometimes, if it had been a hard and wearing day with some annoyance related not usually to the job but to a work mate or to bosses he would come home not even having bothered to wash his face, and it would be smudged with the iron dust and sand and soot where maybe he had brushed his hair out of his eyes or wiped sweat away or rubbed an itching nose.

He rode his bicycle clumsily in those great hard boots, pressing on the pedals with the instep, swaying from side to side as he pedalled, letting that dead tired weight force the pedal down itself without any conscious effort himself, it seemed. The hat was particularly distinctive – because, I think most men coming home from work like that wore caps, or if they were railwaymen, peaked caps. And as he came nearer and I could no longer hope it wasn't him but some similarly looking similarly employed person, I felt sick and frightened. And I stood there thinking desperately, on my own, while the prefect leaned on the lamp-post looking at nothing. I can remember the green lamp-post and his white collar and his blue athletics team blazer and his dark grey trousers.

Once very young I saw where my father worked and I had the impression of a huge hangar with men crouched on the floor in dust and sand heaps and great cylindrical metal structures – boilers or furnaces – and the whole place dim with swirling choking darkness. And two large doors that slid open wide. And that wide exit I remembered especially because I must have been glad to be out. And except for that I didn't see it until years and years later, one day when he forgot his sandwiches for midday so I went down with them. And I went down nervously and terrified because of the previous years of never having gone – he hated it and kept it separate just as much as my mother hated it and kept it away. It was so odd asking for my father by his Christian name. And I walked in so unsure of myself and so conscious of the accent I had lost, and I felt conscious of never having been there before, except that very distant once. They fetched him and he was so pleased and so surprised and so shy, because it showed that at last I had gone there; and yet also he so hated the place, hated having spent his life there when so clearly he should have done such better more congenial things; but I think his dislike of the place was subordinate to his pleasure that I had come to where my father and my grandfather and my great uncle had worked their lives. And he showed me parts of that great hell-like hall, and we climbed up a metal staircase perhaps for boiler inspection or getting to the overhead cranes, so he could show me the view from the roof, the view of the great hideous expanse of corrugated iron roofing and chimney, of lightless factories and still canal, of terrace on terrace of slum housing and squalid corner shop. That though was later.

If I spoke to him the prefect would know he was my father. I wasn't subtle enough then just to have said 'Hello' and pretended it was someone I vaguely knew. Or maybe I didn't want it to be known I even knew, well, such people. So, D., as there was a sight only of the prefect's country bus, a sight of it well beyond the previous bus stop and no possibility of its arriving in time so, D., I turned from the stop, turned towards the antique shop on the other side of the pub, and looked in its window, groping in my pocket as if to find money – and I found in that pocket a halfpenny, I remember – with which to buy something. I wasn't even subtle, D. I didn't even walk on to the next stop so as to speak to my father a few yards away from the school. And he cycled past and the prefect carried on looking at nothing.

That's all, really, that I want to tell you. I got home before my father, which made me hope at first that I had made a mistake and that it hadn't been him. But he had stopped at his sister's on the way, and perhaps it was she who persuaded him to take a 'reasonable' view. He never said anything to me, but as I sat in the front room with my eyes on my book and my stomach sick and any impossible hope that he might not have noticed me so clearly not there, I heard through the wall his talking to my mother, and he was furious. He had, I think, nearly stopped. And I was terrified at all the things that might have happened then. But he hadn't stopped.

It was impossible for me to apologise, impossible for me even to admit that it had occurred. And he never told me he knew. But he must have known I knew he knew. I can't remember what happened, what red silences there were that night. And, D., I don't know if he still remembers this; for ages afterwards I did, vividly. And when I was in the sixth form and used to leave school later in the evenings, I often caught up with him cycling home and I would cycle with him, despite his annoying slowness, as an attempted atonement but it was no atonement, and even writing Iron-moulder for my father's occupation on the entry form to my college at Oxford, in no way replaced that early attitude, that early disavowal.

Gypsies

Down at my grandmother's house, near the river, the gypsies came by and sold us pigeons' eggs. I don't remember if we ate them. Maybe we blew them, pricking a pinhole in each end and blowing out the white and the yolk and keeping the shell to start a collection. It was called Diglis down there, because the land used to belong to the cathedral, *d'église*, in the language of our Norman conquerors. But by the time my grandmother lived there, the land between the old Victorian houses and the river was used as a garbage tip to raise its level so it wouldn't flood each year. And along the riverbank were huge petroleum storage tanks.

The gypsies came to the new house where we lived the other side of the city, upstream, and tried to sell us clothes pegs – big, old style clothes pegs. They would carve two white pegs of wood from the hedgerow and bind them at the top with a strip of metal, and the two legs of this little manikin would clamp down on both sides of the sheet on the clothes lines, the crotch gripping tight. Allegedly, the gypsies left signs on gateposts, secret hieroglyphics indicating where a housewife was good for a cup of tea or in the market for pegs. They carried the pegs in big wickerwork baskets, which they made from the willows that grew down in the withies.

They would come for the picking season, peas and beans and plums and potatoes. Then they would go, no longer wanted. Some of the pubs in town had signs in the windows: 'No Cider No Gipsies.' Sometimes they read 'No Cyder No Gypsies.' The women wore long skirts, and scarves round their heads; their faces were browned and wrinkled from the weather and their mouths had sunk in where their teeth had gone. 'They're not real gypsies,' people would say. Real gypsies spoke Romany and ate hedgehogs baked in clay. We bought out clothes pegs from Woolworths', machine cut, new style, joined together with a coiled wire spring. Someone found that blind people could make wickerwork baskets quickly and cheaply so we bought our wickerwork baskets in support of the blind. Now we use plastic pegs that snap and plastic bags that tear, because that's all there is.

But before the monopolies had absolutely won, the gypsies helped me look for my watch up at the horse boat. It was called the horse boat from those days when horse-drawn barges used to go along the river. An old barge had been moored there for the swimmers. But the moored barge had rotted away and the towpath had crumbled from the wash of the motorised barges they used for transporting petroleum. You could no longer walk all the way down the river meadows to the city and on through to my grandmother's house. Not many people went to the horse boat anymore; not many people even knew of the spot, which is why I'd left my watch beside my clothes.

Two gypsy boys helped me look for the watch I couldn't find when I got out of the water. We must all have been about thirteen. 'It's got a good ticker,' they said, spinning the rear wheel of my bike as it lay on the ground by the river. Tick-tick-tick-tick it went as they spun it round. It had a Sturmey-Archer three-speed hub gear, that was why the wheel ticked as it spun. They were more interested in the ticking than in looking for the watch and it irritated me that they put so much stress on the ticking which had nothing to do with the qualities of the bike.

I would go swimming up at the horse boat on summer evenings. It made my parents happy to think I took an interest in manly activities. So I would cycle up to the horse boat and swim around in the river and lie on the bank and read a book and hope for girls, girls in motorboats, girls in canoes, girls on bicycles, girls on horseback, but there never were any.

Somebody must have given me the watch. Maybe it had been Dad's and didn't keep time properly. Neither Mum nor Dad wore a watch anymore. But everyone else around seemed to be getting them and I wanted to enter that world. This went on for years. I bought a watch at Hong Kong airport and got hassled by customs coming back into Heathrow. They told me how they knew I'd lied; the back of the watch was shiny new; they get rubbed and scratched after they've been worn awhile. I'd felt no better in front of the policeman who brought the gypsy boys and their toothless mother round for identification. They seemed to be the boys. But there was no watch. The mother kept up a harangue of abuse and denial. I never heard what happened.

I did once meet a gypsy girl. That was when I was eighteen, nineteen, hitching from home back to Oxford and gypsies stopped to pick me up in the middle of nowhere in the Cotswolds.

'I was imagining you making love to me beneath an old blanket on the straw in the back of the caravan while the horse clip-clopped through the hedgerows, and I was your gypsy girl,' said Lily. 'Imagine if I'd met you then.'

'It was a Bedford van,' I said. 'General Motors' UK operation. There weren't many horse drawn caravans around when I was hitching. They just stopped to give me a lift. They didn't kidnap me. They didn't steal my heart. They let me out at Oxford and I said goodbye to the gypsy family and their gypsy daughter. I did try to wear a watch again, and silver chains around my neck. But the watches would never keep time as they never kept time for my father. And the chains would blacken and snap. We were a family of puritans and iconoclasts on Dad's side. Cromwell stabled his horses in the cathedral cloisters in the Civil War. So I gave up trying to wear watches and chains and things like that.'

'Maybe they gave you a secret charm when they gave you the lift and you didn't realise it,' Lily said, 'and it's taken all this time to take effect.'

Jealous of Ali

That there was an outside world of prostitutes and sex was brought to me mainly I suppose by people like Alastair. Ali and the other boarders had this air of sophistication – un-provincial I would call it now, but then there was no other world but the provincial to envisage. Ali told stories of an existence different from mine, but it never amounted to a whole way of life I could ever have imagined myself in. I didn't doubt that existence, I could picture it, with Ali's information, vividly. But it was a world I couldn't see myself walking through. It was Ali's world peopled by characters and mapped by landmarks with which he was wholly familiar and which I had never encountered and which I felt I never would.

Going swimming, we used to walk out of the back gate of the school in a sort of column, two-abreast under near discipline, and it was on one such occasion as we approached the single-storey prefabricated huts of the motor taxation offices that I remember the first mention of prostitutes. I hated going to the baths although I could swim. Ali in this as everything was doggedly proficient. More doggedly, perhaps, looking back. But whereas I remember only once in the whole time of visiting the baths ever struggling breathlessly to the deep end and in a panic back, Ali refused to show any fear but bobbed happily from the surface to the deep blue floor of the diving pit holding his nose to keep out the chlorinated water, gesturing obscenely with his free hand.

The revelation of prostitutes enthralled me. Ali gave me convincing documentation. But we were both puzzled by the existence of male prostitutes of whose existence he swore. But why? I remember insisting. And we came to the conclusion that maybe women felt a sexual urge that had to be gratified by financial payment. It seemed to us a very pleasant and lucrative job, and we considered this as, not exactly a future profession, but at least as part of a world that we had not yet really encountered. And we fantastically discussed the possibilities until, approaching nearer the baths, we had to stop in order to appear decorously in our bathing trunks.

Of the as yet un-encountered world, Ali had far more acquaintance than I had. There were perhaps eighty boarders in a school of six hundred, and all of them brought the hint of a world beyond the confines of our Midland hills. Their skins even were different; they seemed to dress differently, in the same conventional school uniform. And they stuck together very much. Boarders were a genus apart. They had a distinctive house spirit, took their mid-morning break in the boarding house while we in our class-room sucked our milk, and they went on walks together on Sundays, when I helped dig up potatoes or mow the lawn at home. To make a friend of a boarder, I felt, was an achievement.

It was a friendship begun, as far as I remember, by Ali's kicking me from the seat behind in a divinity lesson; and this set the tone of our relationship. And if our disregard for established religion caused continual trouble and was a factor in his eventual expulsion, the kicking from behind was the stimulus that awoke me from my Midland terror. Not only did he bruisingly insist that there was another world, but I began to realize it was a world I would have to acknowledge. As we threw board rubbers at each other in later arguments, or slung each other's books around with a fury caused solely by mental disagreements, taken personally, it was this other world I was drawn to approach. Home was one thing, school another, separated by a cycle ride; but Ali asserted a further choice. And London, where in his fifty years my father had never been, began to achieve an insistent possibility. It wasn't that there was any distinction in the fact of Ali's parents' being divorced – this seemed curiously, perhaps, irrelevant; but it was his knowledge of Richmond Park and Leicester Square, Piccadilly Circus and Golders Green; his insistence that film was a serious art form – and my parents never went to the cinema, and discouraged me from going. Sitting next to him I caught a sense of his quicker way of looking at things. I dodged through heavy traffic more easily, and surrendered myself to the terror of underground tube trains. I breathed the whisky fumes of his father, and borrowed Ali's keen teeth to jibe at divinity. We turned our attention to politics as well as biblical exegesis, and found both in Tom Paine. I tried to wean him away from rugby and cricket at which I was impossible and he competent. I failed in that, but it was due to him that I took communion only once after being confirmed, and due to him, some years later, that I dropped a girl I had gone through hours of waiting to get to know, because he insisted her hair looked as if it had been cut with a pudding basin.

His accounts of the sexual delights of Hyde Park, at that stage unexperienced by him, kept me eager with excitement. He lied unscrupulously, but his lies were essentially true; at least essentially valuable. Again, they brought into focus potentialities unimaginable in my home life of homework and bicycle repairs. Our inseparable friendship, as it became, was disliked and instructions were filtered through to me, accounts of his subversive criminality and implications of undisclosed things. This only made the bond the stronger, the appeal the greater, the effect on me the more important. Our prose styles improved with a new self-consciousness of being separate beings in a hostile world, artists alienated from the imperceptive mass. And it was true, for that was how we felt and how we acted; and if we stimulated the world to greater hostility – as if, for us, its hostility was not convincing enough – the greater we noticeably and self-satisfiedly thrived.

And after each holiday he would arrive laden with gifts from the untravelled regions, accounts of an existence that made my own running errands and getting up late cringe for what they were.

And in the arched hall, with the school's benefactor looking down on us in his plus-fours, standing legs apart on a tiger-skin rug, Ali would begin his whispered reports from his world; either there, or after school ended at four, when we would sit in the sun on one of the wooden seats outside the science building – seats presented in memory of people who had fallen dead in some unremembered battle, that had Ali and I noticed, we would have felt it incumbent upon us to despise – he would narrate exoticisms of his distant holiday and, as I was even then aware, lie of un-encountered events.

It was under the arched roof, as we sat officially working on our own at the benched tables running the length of the hall, that Ali told me how some elderly man had tried to pick him up in a tube train; and the roof of the hall lowered, we all sat there in a long row, compartmented by the four tables, and the benefactor looking vaguely towards us as he gripped one of the leather thongs hanging from the roof and swayed there with the rocking carriage, and Ali told how the grey-haired man leant across to him, just as I leant across the better to hear the whisper, and, as it would have been put, engaged him in conversation. And whether the elderly man put his hand on Ali's knee, or this was merely suggested by Ali's power of implication, I forget. But at the next tube-station – and to me then tube-stations were unknown and I refused to inquire of their appearance from Ali – Ali left, and the man followed him, and followed him – Ali all the while peering out of the corner of his eye and over his shoulder and through the masses of cosmopolitan people – into another carriage at another platform, and inside the swaying train – and we swayed across from the benches the better to hear the lowered voice, and the benefactor stood, his seat surrendered no doubt to some lady, aloof and refusing to listen in on someone else's private conversation, the elderly man this time sat next to Ali and perhaps nudged his bare knee – we were still in short trousers – with his own suited one, and said something about 'Ah well, here we are again, fancy that.' No doubt he asked Ali his name, and whether he was doing anything and would he like to be shown round London; and I found it impossible to estimate Ali's response. Did he play up to this? He would not, as I most certainly would, have cringed into himself and fallen silent; no, Ali would no doubt in his turn have engaged the man in conversation; and it was a thought upsetting, that Ali would have responded to the distasteful elderly figure who held a brown paper carrier bag, and I felt what must have been a sort of jealousy; if only I could have envisaged Ali's response. But that image refused to develop, and meanwhile Ali continued the story; he got out at the next station, and the man, after the minimum requisite interval got out too, to stand waiting on the platform. But Ali, who had insisted to me that film, and especially what I now refer to as the B feature thriller, was a form seriously to be considered, leapt through the automatically closing doors the instant they began to slide together, and the tube moved out of the station, with Ali's white face looking through the grimed window at the elderly man standing alone with his carrier bag.

When the bell rang we surged out beneath the tiger's claws into the open morning, the light flooding through the wide doors into that dark hall as if washing across undeveloped film. I kept the fading image with me as I began my ten-minute cycle-ride home – it was no day to break the seven and three quarter minute record – bearing sufficient of its vividness. But I suspected its truth. And I needed to suspect its truth. Yet if it were all fictitious, so that there was no response at all from Ali to such a man, then all his stories of his London of prostitutes and strip clubs and Spanish girls feeding pigeons in Trafalgar Square and pornographic libraries were disqualified too. If it were not true, I had been cheated of a message from the outside, I had been given a glimpse of a world of tube-trains and escalators, that was torn away from me, the poster stripped off to reveal some familiar scene; and I needed to be told that London and sex, no matter what London and what sex, existed; I needed assurance of that life which cycling to and from school four times a day could never encounter. And if it were true, if it were true, then there was a rapport between Ali and the man that my mind could not envisage. Weaving my way through the parked vans and moving cars, past the shops and out towards the flat expanse of the suburbs, the same daily uneventful ride varied only by running occasionally into the back of a bus, I carried with me my choice. And I reflected, cycling along, that no old man had ever tried to pick me up from my quiet world, and I felt jealous of Ali.

Three Incidents for a Mercia Quartet

I can remember the incident now. And anything remembered so long it's fair to suspect carries some unrevealed meaning. Perhaps it was our last sixth form party or the first old boys' dinner. Something rather formal in the school hall, the benefactor looking down on us from his portrait high on the wall, feet spread apart on that tiger skin. All males, all-male school. And here were these token females from the girls' school. And I was talking to Marian who was pale and interesting and artistic, about *The Alexandria Quartet*, that burst of the exotic into our dutiful pursuit of English literature, modern fiction, good books. The light, polished wooden panels attended Marian admiring the bravery of one of our titled actors for being homosexual. And I was wafting off turning this small town into Alexandria, featuring the exotic eye-shadowed girlfriend of a class-mate of mine; he drove her around in a three-wheeler Morgan runabout. What fantasies I could weave about her.

There were locales as bleak as any duck shoot you could imagine, up river where the island was, and all around water meadows and wildfowl, the island where the citizens hid out after flaying a couple of Danish tax-gatherers alive, and the skin was still there in a display case in the cathedral. The exotic tripped readily off the inner pen. The best books, the evanescent never written ones, unheard melodies. It had got to me, that language of desire, and I knew it wasn't Alexandria I was to go to because that was written now and I knew it wasn't just a matter of turning this small town into some pornotropica, it was finding somewhere else.

The other incident was just Marian and me and our bicycles; those inflexible intrusions from the world of the absurd that we had yet to discover and find we had lived. A gravelled driveway up to a country house, past a row of civil defence sheds. Cover your windows with white of egg and sit under the table. It had an almost religious simplicity, this advice on how to survive man's greatest technological triumph of destruction yet. Greatest that we knew of, anyway. Later we began to realise there were many more worse things than we were aware of.

If our bicycles came between us, no less did our navy gabardine raincoats or our plastic yellow cycling capes. We stood, we talked. I didn't want to do the wrong thing and offend, so I did nothing which maybe offended more than anything, and yet there again maybe didn't. These sites of adolescent anxiety, why revisit them?

And the third and final episode, with me in the driveway between our house and next door, a draughty passage just wide enough to get a car down to the garage, and against those wooden creosoted doors between the whitewashed stuccoed walls I'm practising tennis, could it be, belting the ball against the garage doors, the sort of thing to drive everyone mad. And I'm only doing it out of a forlorn and wretched sense of duty, something expected of me, isn't that what it was, make a man of you, good at games, etc. And Marian and her parents pass by on a walk. My parents must have been there too, gardening at the front of the house. Brief dialogue. And me, silent as the grave, etc. She wrote me a note: 'Why?'

Because, you see, her grandfather had been the hated foreman, the loathed and detested bane of my father's and his father's life. What could I do? Admit to dating the foreman's granddaughter?

And it wasn't even that strong a class line, not like I would have liked it to have been to understand it later. There was a detestation apart from the foreman's role, whereas Dad had always liked the boss's son who killed himself when the foundry began to fail, and Dad always said that it was unreasonable pricing by some of the men that led to the collapse that caused all that, and it was one of the things that deeply saddened him.

Lonely boys belting tennis balls at walls and doors, windy grey weekends, green drainpipes with loops of old greyed string where lines had once been strung and broken, sad grey manhole covers and pale concrete, and sparrows twittering from the roof gutters. And maybe the hope of once in a while an interesting aircraft overhead.

War and Pacifism

Back in England back in time, a memory theatre of growing up there, all the struggles and resistances after the new world sense of freedom, back to accent, class, place.

How far back do you want to go? How much about childhood do you want to read? Running across the road in front of a convoy of tanks. A childhood of wartime: though not of war. It wasn't an episode I ever remembered myself, though I was told about it a few times. A few times: it didn't have the status of myth, nothing had the status of myth. My father's favourite book of the Bible was Ecclesiastes. It was not a good basis for parental support in the material world of capitalism red in tooth and claw. All is vanity. Myth a lie. Success unattainable, or if attained evanescent, corrupted. My father's favourite hymn was 'The day thou gavest, Lord, is ended, The darkness falls at thy behest.' We waited for the darkness. It always came.

'It was my gesture of opposing war,' I used to say, later, in my CND days. The war was remote. It hadn't impinged on us in its violence. I would hurtle down the garden path and scurry into the house when flights of aircraft came low overhead, off to bomb Coventry, or to intercept the bombers. Later I would hurtle out of the house to try and read the registration numbers on the wings or fuselage. But that was after the war. We used to get booklets that had lists of all the serial numbers of Midland Red buses, one after the other. When we saw a bus we would underline the serial number in the book. We tried collecting aircraft serial numbers too, but it wasn't often they flew low enough to read the registrations. I tried to compile my own master list, the registration of every aircraft that had ever flown. I had the letters, all I needed were the makes and marks of the aircraft themselves. Did it count if you saw the registration in a film or television? We didn't have television or often go to films. Sometimes I would see a serial number on the fuselage of an aircraft being taken by articulated lorry along the main road. Did a fragment count, a substantial fragment?

I would fly myself to bed at night, taking off from the dining room table in a twin-engine Dinky, vroom vroom, climb up the stairs, bank round the landing, land in the bathroom, refuelling stop while I cleaned my teeth, then take off again from the ceramic shelf beneath the mirror, off to bed.

For a while the prisoners of war had hoed in the fields at the back of the house, thin, stooped men in ill-matched clothes, hoeing away amidst the stones and crops.

My father had been too young for the First World War and too old for the second. And he was working in a protected industry, old enough for that, leaving school at twelve. And there was a strong anti-militarist spirit in the family. My grandfather had refused to work Saturdays during the First World War because, at that point, he was a Seventh Day Adventist, which took some sticking out, my father said, not working on Saturday in the war. So there was a generally anti-war line. When it came to joining the school cadet force, one of the rites of puberty, I said I wasn't going to.

'Why not?' my father said.

'I'm a pacifist.'

There was a book in the house, *Vain Glory*, about the slaughter of the First World War, and I would read it to fuel my stand. It was a stand my parents were not very sympathetic to. This on top of trying to evade school games all the time. I was a bit torn. I would have liked to have gone into the air-force cadets and spotted aircraft. But you had to go through the army cadets first. Doing drill in the playground Friday afternoon, blancoing belts, brassoing buckles. There wasn't much pressure. 'I'm against militarism,' I explained to the commanding officer.

'Well, I'm not sure joining the corps is militarism.'

'I think it is,' I said.

I was drafted to the gardening squad, weeding the flowerbeds outside the headmaster's Georgian house. It was a predominantly lower-class crew. Not high-minded idealists there, I was sad to find out. Not the sensitive poets writing critiques of the system, but C-stream boys from working class families, not the aristocracy of labour but the resistant, sceptical, cynical non-collaborators, skivers, dodgers, idlers, those who refused to do a decent day's work, those who did not take on the school spirit, a work gang of the marginalised, the malingerers, the delinquent, not officer-material. Had I really thought it would have put me with the idealists given belated recognition and carved in marble and laid in shrines?

Then I was plucked out of the gardening squad and seconded to the school secretary. There were a couple of other boys from the year ahead in the same position. They worked the duplicating machine.

'The machine-gun of the revolution,' said Gordon.

They ran off documents the secretary gave them, put on stencils, loaded the ink tubes, wiped down the machine. They made inventories of the book-store. Locked away in it, Gordon would take in hand my political education, his glasses dropping down his button nose and pushed back up again with his forefinger as he giggled at some administrative absurdity in the school.

I wasn't trying to be an outsider. I wanted to be loved, respected, accepted. I did the tasks efficiently. I proof-read the school prize-giving program. First step into applied literary ability, first participation in the machinery of literary production. I found that the school's motto, *sperno mutare*, I spurn to change, had been printed *spermo mutare*, so I corrected it and felt proud of detecting error in an official document and of satisfactorily fixing it up for authority.

'Damn,' said Gordon, unpacking the bundles of prize-giving programs. 'They noticed.'

'They couldn't have,' said John.

'Noticed what?' I asked.

'We changed the motto last year but they've gone and changed it back again. We thought we'd introduced a bit of obscenity for at least a decade. *Spermo mutare* is so much more suggestive, don't you think?'

I blushed.

'Oh, we didn't know you were so sensitive.'

I blushed easily. But I said nothing. I felt stupid. I tried to persuade myself I'd done the right thing, correcting error, minutely scrutinising for mistakes. But I felt stupid. I was not a natural anarchist though I was beginning to recognise the appeals of subversion. I felt negative, reactive, undoing the achievements of the creative imagination. And I felt guilty, not admitting that I was the one who had made the change. But I couldn't admit it, I would look so stupid and puritanical and conformist. I could imagine Gordon's reaction: 'You should apply for late admission into the army corps. You're missing your vocation here.'

The Midlands. 'O pastoral heart of England,' Quiller-Couch intoned on Eckington Bridge. 'The dead centre,' we intoned sardonically. We wanted to get away and if you couldn't get away you could imagine that there was somewhere else that existed and one day you might get to it.

A. E. Housman, for instance. *A Shropshire Lad*. He wasn't a Shropshire lad, the English master, old Bill, told us, he was a Worcestershire lad. Shropshire was that somewhere else he could look across to, the next county. 'In summertime on Bredon... My love and I would lie, And see the coloured counties.' Counties. In the plural. Not just one, but others, there were others.

My father and grandfather had always read a lot. Grandfather had been liable to take days off work to read Walter Scott and Fenimore Cooper. That was deemed excessive. But reading was an approved activity. I wanted to be able to do something approved. So I read books to dream of other lives and got locked onto the idea of the books themselves as much as any lives they described; the lives I especially liked were the lives of books, the artist as a young man, the artist emergent, I would be a writer.

'If you were going to be a writer you'd have written books by now,' my mother said.

'There's no money in being a writer,' said my father.

I took no especial notice of them, it was no different from their reactions to anything else. It was depressing and demoralising but that was no different either. And having taken up my position, I locked myself into it. That was it. A writer.

With the skills acquired at the duplicator we started a magazine, Ali and I, Ali another dissident who had refused to join the corps. We called it *Grendel*. A monster defeated by the first English epic hero could not be all bad. It wasn't utterly clear whether we were on the side of the defeated or the monsters. I suspect that Ali preferred the monsters. But already we had rejected the heroes along with the other leaders, warriors, sportsmen.

We designed it as an alternative to the official school magazine, undercutting it in price, offering more contentious and topical material. I wrote a story about the compulsory cross-country runs; somebody slipping on the icy towpath of the canal, breaking a limb and freezing to death. Tich, the master in charge of cross-country running said he was sympathetic to our endeavours but some things had to be done and this only made it more difficult. He was a socialist. As far as we knew the only socialist on staff, though that was not the sort of thing, being socialist, staff members would have publicised.

Tich told us about the architecture of banks. The reason banks had huge granite blocks facing the street and framing their doorways was to give the illusion of solidity in order to lure you to deposit your money with them. It was a revelation, that architecture was an ideology, that bricks and mortar and granite blocks were a rhetoric, that the concrete was an illusion. This was at the time that banks no longer built with granite blocks but projected a modern image of steel frames and glass curtain walling.

Revelations are always about the old; the present ever awaits demystification. And in the Midlands we still lived in the past, amidst the provincial banks and the narrow workers' cottages. 'Look at the doorways of working people's houses, a slit in a wall to crawl home through, and compare that with the great porticos of the banks. What does that tell you about society?' Now my environment became fraught with significance, the social embedded in the visual. When I set my lonely protagonists in a story now, the rows of houses conveyed the message of social oppression, the proud porticoes the aggressions of power and money and status.

We sold *Grendel* along the morning bun queue when the school lined up to buy doughnuts or dripping cakes or buns to eat with their free milk. We financed a second issue by selling advertisements round shops in town. If some shops bought space under the illusion it was the official magazine they were supporting, it was not from explicit deception. But it helped the finances. After the second issue we liquidated the venture and spent the profits on buying a batch of Penguins and Pelicans and dividing them between us. I bought one on modern architecture and learned about modernism and functionalism and swallowed the claim that these styles were not only new but real, modern and true, honest. No more phoney granite blocks. All was now straight lines, Le Corbusier rectangles. The rest of the profits Ali spent on subscribing to the ultra-right wing neo-Nazi National Party. It was oppositional, like *Grendel*; and monstrous, like Le Corbusier. Since he was a boarder at the school, he used my address for his subscription. My father complained bitterly at what the mail delivered.

On the Road to Stratford

Membership of the Adam Lindsay Gordon Society was a step on the path of literary aspiration. We stayed back after school under the tutelage of the English master and read from our own work in a deserted classroom. But the invitation to the Shakespeare Reading Society was the mark of acceptance, reading from the works of Shakespeare on a Sunday evening in the Headmaster's house. This was the entrée to the higher world of culture and French words. French windows, too, opening out onto the croquet lawn from the long, low Georgian house, the trace of medieval monastic ruins beyond the grass at one end, the stand of horse chestnut trees at the other, and the Headmaster intoning Hamlet, Prince Hal, Lear, Macbeth, Othello. This was as the world would be, privilege, exclusivity: and the girls from the private school over the wall brought in to read the few girls' parts. Knees together on the long, low couch. The Headmaster opposite in his arm chair. We attendant lords from the sixth form on straight-backed, hard, auxiliary seating.

'It is his attempt to demonstrate that he is not a philistine,' said Gordon.
    The attendant lords discuss the Head.
    'In this, as in all else, he fails,' said John.

'A career built securely on the sure foundations of failure,' said Gordon.

Gordon was chubby, snub-nosed, cynical, beyond illusion, the son of refugee German Jews. John was local working-class, lived too near the back gate of the school so everyone could place him in his proletarian context. They were the outsiders who, no less than the Headmaster, were concerned to demonstrate that they were not philistines. Far from it. Not aesthetes, not like Kemp who wore his overcoat loose over his shoulders like a cloak and sported a carnation. They found Kemp as amusing as the Head. Non-sporting, non-members of the Officer Training Corps, they controlled entry to outsiderdom. They transformed exclusion into exclusivity, and if you wanted to participate in that you had to knock on their door.

The Headmaster had been a runner. Not much else was known about him. Nothing said, anyway.

'He is certainly not known as a scholar,' said Gordon.

But he had run in the Berlin Olympics.

'We cannot blame the rise of the Third Reich on his failure in the 440 yards,' said Gordon.

'But we will,' said John.

'Ah yes, we will,' said Gordon. 'His capitulation to Nazi might prefigured the ignominy of appeasement.'

Under the banner of pacifism they refused to join the Officer Training Corps, but that did not prevent their decrying appeasement. I absorbed the contradictions silently. If they were contradictions. So many issues never seemed to become clear.

'Do we imply,' said Gordon, 'that he was suborned by Nazi gold to throw the race? And to assure Hitler that he had nothing to fear from Britain?'

'Or was he suborned by Churchill to throw the race, and to lure Germany into aggression, so Churchill could have his finest hour?' suggested John.

'Why not both?' suggested Gordon. 'Why should we imagine he was so scrupulous as to take money from only one side?'

'But where has the money gone?' asked John. 'Where are the evidences of wealth beyond Swiss dreams?'

'Blackmail?' suggested Gordon. His eyes twinkled. It was a delightful thought. Behind the Georgian façade, behind the drawn curtains, the Headmaster sits at his desk, his head in his hands, another letter of demand fallen to the carpet.

'Or the Rolls-Royce.'

'Oh, it must be the Rolls-Royce,' said Gordon.

It was the Headmaster's splendid assertion. That and playing the French horn in the school concerts. Badly, Gordon would insist, don't funk out on the adverb. And intoning Hamlet, Prince Hal, Lear, Macbeth, Othello etc. The Rolls.

An old Rolls. It was still possible to pretend, at that time, that an old Rolls was the best Rolls.

But this 1924 model? No, the pretence was sad. All of a piece with the bad, balding Hamlet, the risible white-face Othello.

It stood on the gravel sweep before the Georgian façade.

'He gets his wife to push it out of the garage first thing in the morning,' the boarders claimed, or at least the dissident ones. 'The battery's flat and it won't start. So they push it. She got the milkman to help her last time.'

'Or is the Rolls the cover?' said Gordon. 'To conceal the fact of the blackmail? Indeed the blackmailers may have blackmailed him into buying the Rolls at a grossly inflated price as part of their scheme.'

It seemed not impossible.

Nothing seemed impossible. Not after an invitation to the Shakespeare Reading Society.

So there I sat. Waiting on my half-dozen lines. The anxiety of the debut. The agony of the straight-backed un-cushioned chair. And around me polite manners, art and culture, private school girls. All that you could ever desire in England. There it all was encapsulated. Authority, status, art, sex, the inextricables, the future. And the Headmaster declaiming 'Oh that this too too solid flesh would melt' in his sensitive, strangulated vowels. To show us how to speak. Though there was no attempt at formal instruction, no lesson in elocution. It was as if he felt that we were what we were and it was best not to put a veneer of anything superior on this dull, resentful, provincial backwater. That way, Headmasterly superior distance was preserved.

For it was superiority he projected, the ruling class descending on this Midland outpost. And how could we see then, with no experience, no bearings, no points of comparison, that this was just the sad pretension of the under usher, the hired hand? He had taught at a minor public school before becoming our Headmaster. Just one of the lackeys of the system. That perhaps was why he was so cut off, so fractured, so neurotically unapproachable.

But he presented, and it was accepted, an image of the superior being, come to civilise this country bumpkin grammar school. He was not loved for it. Nor was there anything to respect. His Henry V was delivered to a room of Falstaff's cronies, young of heart and body but full of resentment beyond their years. His Hamlet was assessed with the clear cold vision of the English master's gravedigger, Gordon's and John's Rosencrantz and Guildenstern. Hearing his Othello our sympathies embraced Iago, admiring someone who could so effortlessly bring such an icon down. In Lear his ravings seemed typecast, despite a lack of grandeur or gravitas.

'The reason he invites in girls from next door to play the female parts is not only to discourage incipient transvestism,' said Gordon, 'but to prevent the enthusiasm with which we would play Goneril and Regan. Our contempt and loathing would be too apparent. What wouldn't you give for a shot at Lady Macbeth?'

Outside the French windows the midges and gnats spiralled in their dance of death. The hedgehogs snuffled for worms at the lawn's edge. Come into the garden, Maud. But the girls sat in an unapproachable row. When the headmaster's wife brought in the execrable coffee in the minute English porcelain cups the Headmaster and the English master fraternised with the young ladies. We other ranks sat rigid on the upright chairs, all effort concentrated into not spilling, not dropping, not breaking the fragile cups rattling on their fragile saucers.

Oh art, oh culture. Oh literature. Was it better than crouching over the radio, listening to the Third Programme late at night, the sound turned down to its lowest so as not to keep my father awake who had to rise at six for his job, physical labour, filth and grime, real work, the cultural mission of the BBC, noble as it proclaimed itself, broadcast too late for such proletarian, licence-payers to appreciate? One way or another culture, that liberation of the human spirit to which I aspired, into which I wished to soar and fly and be absorbed, involved a lot of discomfort. A discomfort inextricably linked with class, class perceptions, class roles, class possibilities. I might have learned from that. Or I might have suppressed it. Or I might have suppressed it and learned subconsciously. The slow incubation of an English disease. No wonder I followed Adam Lindsay Gordon to Australia.

It was on the road to Stratford that the headmaster's Rolls broke down.

'Probably the very spot that Shakespeare stopped to have a piddle,' said Gordon.

The Forest of Arden, or the razed remnants of its perimeter, stretched out beneath us to one side. On the other, traffic whizzed by. The Headmaster's voice got higher and wheezier, choked with emotion and exhaust fumes.

'Maybe it's the carburettor, sir,' said John. 'Did these old models have carburettors, sir?'

The Headmaster walked away from our help.

'Maybe it's out of petrol,' said Gordon. 'Maybe the money he collected for petrol was to pay the blackmailers.'

Yes, the Headmaster had collected contributions for petrol from his impoverished proletarian and refugee charges. I found it unbelievable. No less unbelievable than my father found it. On that salary. But I paid up. We always paid up.

It was my first lesson in the household economics of the bourgeoisie. Until then I had believed impoverishment and penny-pinching were the unique preserve of the working class. That was their destiny, that was the doom I had to escape. It was a delusion I continued to hold despite this early evidence to the contrary.

The Headmaster fumed. He glared at his watch as he waited for the Royal Automobile Club patrolman to arrive.

'I'm sure we'll get there before the curtain rises, sir,' said Gordon, at his most oleaginously and least persuasively conciliatory.

'It's not the damn play, we'll miss the race,' snapped the Headmaster.

The play was the thing to get us to pay the petrol money. What the Headmaster wanted was to attend the regatta in the afternoon. Cheer on the school boat. Hobnob with other Headmasters from Headmasters' Conference Schools. Park his Rolls beside their Ford Consuls and Standard Vanguards and other such vulgarities of mass production. Before an evening at the Shakespeare Memorial Theatre.

'Maybe we should ask for a refund,' suggested Gordon. 'So we can catch the train back. To be sure of getting home.'

'Lucky we weren't taking the crew, sir,' said John.

The rowers had gone earlier in the rowing master's car and the deputy coach's car. They wouldn't be staying on for any play. We were just the rabble in the Rolls. Stage soldiers to walk round the back and out the front again. No wonder we had to pay for our petrol. We filed past the Rolls, peering in at its open bonnet, and round the back of it, like bad extras, over-acting our concern at the overheated, out-of-petrol, fallen piece of tragic hubris. The Headmaster glowered at us. We walked round again.

'A Ford, a Ford, my Headmastership for an Anglia,' said Gordon.

The Fir Trees

As soon as he saw the house, the father said the fir trees would have to be cut down. They were dying, going an ugly brown; and planted too close together, their sides rubbing against each other, they had no light or air. But they had to be cut down because they were unproductive; even if they had been all green and flourishing, they would have been condemned; their dying was an excuse, not a reason. And when, because of its view and its village, he bought the house, he said the first thing we've got to do is to get down those fir trees. Because they were taking up space and producing nothing. And they were taking the goodness out of the soil; and he could grow nothing next to them; and he couldn't afford to waste land. And as they were dying, the son didn't defend them.

And even before they moved into the house, the son, back home for the summer, helped to cut down the dusty branches and leave the sawn trunks there, bare, letting light onto the potatoes and young sprout plants. It was a gesture of ownership by the father. He had bought the house and now he would force his personality on it; and his way of forcing his personality on it was to destroy traces of the previous one. The branches were sawn off easily. And it was a gesture, too, by the father against the people in other houses in the village, or so the son assumed.

The father had saved in the town. He had denied himself living to save. After the years of austerity he had demonstrated his triumph over his environment by leaving it. As a boy he had always loved the village, had been driven off the Manor with a gun when he had been bird-nesting, had scoured every hedgerow for blackberries, every field for mushrooms. It had been his escape from the town to walk the four miles to the village and fields. Now it was filled with solicitors and schoolmasters, doctors and garage owners, who had built their houses and planted high hedges and sliding cypresses. Cutting down the fir trees was harsh and irrevocable; because he had to show these soft-handed men he had come up the harsh way, that for him life had been saving and denying, and ornamental unproductive trees had no part in it. And though the mother complained and said it made the place look like an allotment, and coming here had been to somewhere where people didn't have allotments, and where successful individuality was shown by high hedges and tall trees and lawns you couldn't see onto, she agreed in the end that the trees were dying and to cut them down would give more garden for vegetables and would economise on coal for the winter.

When they sat eating their meals they looked out of the window onto not houses but a large field at the distant end of which was the Manor. He told these stories of being ordered off the grounds when he was a boy with a sort of delight in days when people could order you off with guns. And looking across at the Manor, he had only an ambivalent pleasure that today no one would brandish a shotgun at a trespasser. He had fought his way out of the fifty years gone past but his acceptance of gains was ambivalent. Those days were hard, he would say. And it seemed that for that reason they were good.

Like axe blows on the trees, those days were clean and harsh. When a few people called to see him in his new house he would show them the trees being cut down and then the views from the other sides, across the field to the Manor. Then he would remember the old days and say it wasn't the same now. The same family lived there still, but the present Squire was a bad egg. Or sometimes he would say simply, he was no good. And saying this

his voice would drop and he would look as if to say, there's a lot goes on there but I wouldn't want my daughter to hear me telling you. Hearing him dropping his voice, the son realised that his father must have heard too; he wished he hadn't as it would mean more hard violence of attitude, a firmer confirmation of the essential rightness of the hard way.

His mother had written, in one of her letters to him at college, that the Squire had married an *au pair* girl. He had opened the letter walking to a cafe for breakfast at about eleven one morning. He skimmed through it in the street, bought a paper which he took in case there was no one to talk to over breakfast, and went to his fried egg, sausage and tomato. As he had only skimmed through the letter, it didn't make much impact. Except to remark as a friend sat at his table, 'The Squire – we're very feudal still at home – seems to have gone and married his *au pair*. Didn't even know he'd got one. Can't think why my mother's mentioned it though.' He referred to her on the few occasions he had cause to refer to her there as 'my mother.' 'Mother' on its own and 'the old lady' belonged to different upbringings, both of which he and his father would have repudiated. Even being away from home for three years hadn't changed his still thinking in small things as his father, things so small he didn't notice them and so never changed them. Later he realised why his mother had mentioned an item of news whose only and contextually unlikely interest was either prurient or 'there but for the grace of God'. They had bought this house near the Manor, the Squire was part of the new field of gossip. And he remembered, too, having coffee one Saturday morning, the year before, those interminable Saturday mornings of vacation, in town and meeting some girl he had been at school with who told him rumours of the Squire's doings. He would come into town with some girl he had picked up and take her to a shoe shop and buy her the most expensive and impractical shoes, and take her round shops, and to restaurants.

Even cutting down trees and helping and participating in the hard way, he still could not avoid clashes with his father. Clashes over which way to push and where the soil should be shovelled from in getting up the trunk and which way it would be best for the branches to crash down. But at least this participation seemed a sign of solidarity to the family.

The father would talk to an old man from a cottage in the village who was a gardener at the Manor. He had been a gardener before the present bad egg inherited. And he would tell the father about girls brought down from London and confirm that the Squire was no good. And the father would occasionally hint at happenings, saying 'people and things staying there' to a visitor as they looked out of the window across the field. And there would be sympathetically censuring nods. And the son would look across at the high fir trees clustering round the Manor, and the birds wheeling round them and in and out of them, and the wind gently rustling the deep blue green of the leaves and see in the composition a symbol, in the almost concealed house, of everything he was at present missing. So the Squire whom on social and political grounds he would have condemned, he held privately as a type of rebel who had evaded his duties and responsibilities and judges, and was living. He saw in him a man desperately clutching at lust not just for itself but as a defiance, too, against his own particular hard way. Not that he worried too much about the marriage; he didn't see the Squire, as he felt sure the Squire saw himself, as carelessly trapped. He was sure, as no doubt the Squire was sure, he would carry on philandering irrespective of his young European wife. But every time the father spoke of the Squire as no good, over the hedge to a friendly passer by or at tea to a relation or visitor, the son felt a defiance and clutched at his myth to live through.

Killing time he redesigned the garden, impressing his own personality on it by digging two flower beds into the lawn, and changing the position of a great stone bird bath. One evening at tea, his father tired after a day's hard work and resenting his son's not doing anything, the son suggested a holly tree in the hedge should be cut down. Along the hedge across which they looked to the field and the Manor were regularly placed holly trees. From where he sat at the tea table, the son could see only the holly tree; it blocked his view of the firs waving and the birds wheeling.

'There's plenty of trees to come down if you want to get them down; you can go and saw that fir up.'

'That's nothing to do with it. This'll come down in a minute.'
'It won't.'
'What do you mean, it won't?'
'Because it isn't.'
'Why not?'
'Because it isn't.'
'But it blocks the view.'
'I can see quite well enough without cutting it down.'

The family sat there still. It happened so often and the merits of each case were rarely important.

'It seems silly to me,' the son said, 'to ruin a view for no reason.'

'I can see quite enough of that place as it is. It's not coming down so that's that.'

And besides, the father had regularity on his side. The row of hollies was evenly spaced. To take out one would upset the row. Outside in the garden the firs sheltering the Manor could be seen; well, it was only from the room that the view was restricted.

Quickly the father settled there, ignoring the fact of doctors and solicitors but talking over the hedge to the old gardener and to the farm labourer working in the field. He walked the fields reliving his childhood blackberrying and childhood holidays. He would say, if his father had had enough money to buy a house like this, how he and his brother and sisters would have loved playing and roaming around in the fields, or playing cricket on the lawn; and the son and daughter who were adjusted to other activities, who were bad at games and bored with country walks and hated the close proximity of the family, sat silent or read. And though the Squire was an evil-living man, sometimes this aspect would seem to be blotted out and the visitor would be told how the Squire had married a young wife and they went past riding together in the early morning. And well they may have done; but the father's picture was imagined in that fifty years back glow where the gamekeeper had carried a shotgun and the Squire and wife would trot by and if you failed to touch your cap you were liable to be kicked. The father, in the evenings the son had omitted to go out, would tell how his own father had refused to open the gate for one such Squire, and in telling these reminiscences he would seem to endorse the validity of the society where such powers and sanctions were held and enforced; in those days it was hard, and men were clean-living.

The son wondered how the Squire had met the girl, he wondered how an *au pair* girl, a girl half his age, could have given herself to that elderly man. He imagined her out on her own, exercising her horses, firm on some beautiful animal passing through the narrow lanes, down to the river and the old mill, up the hill again and to the steep track down to the dingle, past the old farms and half-timbered cottages. He imagined this girl to have come from some bombed and grimy industrial town, and come to learn the language, and had seen her opportunity. He imagined her visualising the horses and the quiet country lanes, narrow and high-hedged and travelled only by the occasional tractor; visualising the rambling house with its mossed roof and the firs sheltering round it; visualising the home of ease and large wood fires, the fields to walk over at will, the expensive cars. Or was she seduced by the ridiculous shoes? One day he caught a glimpse over the hedge of a dark-complexioned, black-haired girl galloping past, just a glimpse of dark hair, a black leather jacket. It must have been her, and he was able to put a face and slender figure to the girl he imagined riding over the hump-backed bridge set at right angles to the road, with perhaps a startled hare running before her, the girl he imagined sitting still on her horse and looking across the country with its many gentle hills as the swallows screeched or the lapwings settled on the fields. The image of her riding round those lanes, and living in the large house which was so dark and which could not be seen from its front or rear gateways, was an image of a sort of vitality, of something standing alive amidst the decaying old gardener and hostile villagers and commuters and the old, good and atrophied hard way.

Having sawn off the branches, they were getting up the stumps of the trees. It was hard. They would dig round and expose strong roots which they would chop at with a heavy axe. The father would swing a pick to loosen the soil and the son shovel out the earth.

The trees had been planted close together so there was little space to work in. They had to work close and there was a danger of these two, not attuned to each other, clumsily swinging an axe or striking a spade against the other. But though they would cry quickly and harshly 'Watch it!' or 'Careful!' and claim nearly to have been hit, there was never any accident. They were too frightened to hurt each other because they knew how much at sudden times they wanted to.

As they dug down deeper each had to stand in the hollow, chopping and shovelling, and always the father would say how nearly they were finished and they never were. The son disliked the work and knew his father thought he hated it. He had to keep on to stop suspicions of his weakness, unmanliness, or after the nights out, unfitness and dissipation. There was always some unspoken accusation. So he struggled and did not stop when the father did, and the blows of the axe were blows at his father's image. Though he could never have smashed any human head like that. But the image he shattered. And the father having had it hard from his youth knew that at least it had made a man of him and that he wasn't afraid of work. And that way they pulled down the trees.

When they had cut off most of the roots they started to dig underneath with the pick; and striking the top of the trunk – sawn off about four feet above the ground – they could shake the whole stem and knew they were near to heaving it over. Sweat poured out of both of them; and the father's sweat was irritating to the son, it was as if the father were deliberately sweating to offend what he imagined as the hypersensitive prejudices in his son, as if deliberately spitting on his son's belief in things other than tree-grubbing and manual work. And so the son sweated less, almost as if suggesting that by an intelligent use of force there was no need to sweat, and also that he could control himself, and suggesting that though he had been away for three years on and off and met friends at night in pubs, his body was in good condition; and he contrived at the same time to despise and dissociate himself from his body, while insisting on its strength and fitness. And having chopped and beaten away most of the roots, they both pushed against the trunk. And the father pushed and pulled so that the tree jerked back at the son and the son suggested they should just push as the wriggling seemed to him clumsy and violent, a brute wrestling, while a planned force would throw over the tree and it seemed as if the father deliberately was asserting the brute wrestling or was so intent on it that he failed to listen to any other suggestion. They pushed, the father's rough heavy hand pushed on the tree and on the son's uncalloused hand; the touch, the continual bumping contact, the sweat, the panting breaths, the brute closeness, affronted him.

And as they struggled, against each other and against the tree and against the planter of the trees, along the metalled road came the sound of horse hooves. Each struggled as if unaware. They were tired, had pushed hard, needed time to breathe but both would not stop until she had gone by. The horse came near, unhurrying. They heaved, as if to have the tree torn out from their aching chests as she passed the gate. And looking as he pushed, the son saw her, dark-complexioned, expressionless, her black hair just showing on her forehead beneath a soft white headscarf worn in some unfamiliar fashion; and this dark vision looked placidly and unmovingly for the brief moment before she was past the angle of the gate, her face expressing nothing communicable, but her presence on the horse affecting those two at the tree stump.

And when she was gone, concealed by the hedge, neither said anything, they both stopped and the son picked underneath the butt of the tree and the father cut down with the spade, and not long afterwards they had the trunk lying against the side of the hole they had dug, it roots torn and burst, and they dragged it away and cut it in two with the saw.

Armistice

So I go to see my aunt to say goodbye again, she is ninety and this could be the last goodbye, my mother has been saying this for twenty years now, it might be the last time you see her, and it never is, but one time it will be, and she tells me the same stories again that I never listen to, having heard them so many times with deaf ears, refusing to listen to their insistent message.

'What have you been doing?' she asks perfunctorily.

'Picking apples,' I say.

'Has your mother got someone to pick the rest of them?'

Always failure, always incompletion, a good job never well done.

'I've got them all,' I say. 'The ones the ladder will reach. It needs a longer ladder than we've got to get the rest.'

'Oh, those young sailors,' she says. 'I'm always terrified when they climb up. I'm always afraid they might slip, they've been trained but they're so young. Four of them climb up in time to the music, those huge high masts, and then the one climbs to the top and they drop the petals. There's a petal for every one of the dead in the two great wars, millions of petals.'

'There would be,' I said.

'I've been remembering my war service,' she said, 'the risks I took.'

In the old people's home the heat pumps through the radiators like Zyklon-B. Dad would never visit there. He couldn't breathe in the heat. I used to think it was just an excuse, a rationalisation for his choice of economy and cold, a resentment against the squander of tax-payers' money. Sure he was dying of emphysema from the years as a moulder. There were good reasons not to visit. Now I sat there and sweltered.

'This soldier was back from the front,' she said. 'He said, you've been here too long, you should go to the war office. He wrote such a well-written letter. It was so good I couldn't send it. I only copied out part of it. Such a nice boy. A public school boy.'

No doubt.

'I volunteered,' she said. 'They only took volunteers. It was a huge big building. And inside were walls, and then more walls, and there were two of you at a time in these little forts. You were locked in your own little fort, just two at a time packing the powder. Then if there was an explosion only the two of you were killed in your own little fort. You were only there for half an hour at a time. If you breathed in the powder for too long at a time you got sick. One time there was a huge explosion. We never knew how many were killed. It was all military secrets. I wasn't there when it happened. Some of the powder had got on my stomach and made me sick and I was off for a few days at home. In the end I had to transfer. The powder was getting on my stomach and making me sick. That was when I went to the war office. I was one of the last five to leave the war office. Those were marvellous times. But I was so frightened cycling home at night. We had to work late and I had to cycle two or three miles from the station, along a country road, and my friend went one side of the Park and I had to go the other, down through a paddock, up and down this bumpy road. I went smack into a cow one night, and then into the barn, and there were no lights, and I had to leave my bicycle in the barn and walk through to the other end and out into the yard. Mother was never game to come and look for me. Someone asked her once wasn't she worried about her daughter having to cycle home alone late through the dark. "I've got four little ones to look after," she said. "I'm so busy getting them all off to bed I don't have time to worry about anything else." I remember this officer on the station one night. "Aren't you afraid to be alone on the station at this time of night?" he said. "Well, it's war work and I volunteered and it has to be done," I said. He was a young public school boy. He was off to the front. There were all sorts of people in the war office; well-educated people, clergymen's daughters and doctors' daughters and solicitors' wives. I did enjoy those times. Do you remember the Banks, they were county people? Mr Banks said something about a battalion and I said, "That's a thousand men." "How did you know that?" he said. "I used to work in military records," I said. He was impressed.'

All those years of refusing to join the school cadet corps, marching for CND, anthologising against the Vietnam war, are they all in vain? Has she never registered them, is she now in a world of her own like she always was, or is this to shame me for not wearing a poppy for Armistice Day, for not being patriotic, for being an expatriate, for not having gone to public school, for her sister's having married an iron-moulder, a job not only proletarian but a reserve occupation, exempting my father from military service. She shows me the long roll of photograph of the war office, seventy years ago, officers, boots, moustaches, hierarchies.

Ah, dear aunt, you taught me about the sub-text, you showed me how narration transmitted ideology, sometimes I even think you helped drive me into exile, you and the world to which you subscribe, the dominant world, the world whose ideas are the dominant ideas, whose art is the dominant art in every age. You proclaimed those values to me, Sunday after Sunday when you came round to tea, and at every opportunity in between. It is only right I should record something of them, those values that thrust me unavoidably if not unambiguously into the ranks of resistance, of refusal, for that alone you deserve our gratitude. The future may be ours but we can afford a moment to remember how the present still belongs to you.

Nephew's Story

The bed-sitting room, the afternoon light streaming through the window, the high-backed easy chair, the dark furniture around the walls, the mementoes, photographs, pot plants, dried flowers, little objects. The little objects I cannot immediately recall. They meant a lot to my aunt, they were the memory theatre of her life, all with their associations. They took her out of the room through space and time. To me they represented the fetishism of objects, they were just clutter. I could afford to reject all that, or thought I could. At the time I felt I had no choice but to reject it, the oppressive weight of the old world, old values, which I had travelled so far to escape. But every time I revisited the objects would all be in place, in still, silent repose.

Not that my aunt was necessarily silent.

'What about our poor boys in Aden being attacked like that?' she greeted me.

I muttered that I didn't see our boys had any justification for being in Aden.

But she would ride roughshod over my mutterings, hearing them yet refusing to hear them, so that every visit was a battle of Empire, a confrontation of politics, of faith, of aesthetics, of haircuts, the lot.

'Oh, I thought you were the man come to mend the boiler,' she greeted me in my denim phase. She didn't have a boiler, of course, whatever a boiler might have been. The denim looked like a boiler suit, or could be held to look like one, the uniform of the working class, that was the only point.

And so the photographs and objects around her room became the memory theatre for me of confrontation, mnemonic icons of the class war, of all the appalling oppression and exploitation and privilege that she was committed to supporting, benefiting from none of it herself. Lady Diana somebody or other in hunting gear, on horseback, a photograph from the 1920s, hung on the wall. I do not immediately remember if the horse was stationary, Lady Diana erect in silhouette; or if it was leaping over a hedge, Lady D. leaning forward along the horse's back. The detail did not matter to me; or, if it did, I refused it. For me it was a simple image of privilege and all the economic and political and social repression privilege bore with it. Here was Lady Diana, daughter of the family to which my aunt's father was head groom, still lording it over us from the wall. It embodied that inalienable distance between the privileged socialite and my aunt, and me too, of course. And yet here was my aunt commemorating that world, Lady Diana's sprawling country house, my aunt in a bed-sitting room.

The resentments were, of course, all mine. To my aunt there were our betters, the upper classes, the aristocracy, and then all the various gradations. For me such a vision was one of injustice and exploitation: to her it was the natural order. Those who advocated change of the order – Labour people, Communists – were wicked. I think that was her word, wicked. It sounds right. But writing this I find how much I can no longer remember. Whether forgotten or repressed, I am not investigating. Those conflicts were so painful I am happy so little remains.

Her bed-sitting room I suppose I saw as an imprisonment, the solitary cell. There were the people she admired, she adulated, living in spacious splendour, and she was reduced to the one small room. But I don't know that she felt that way about it. She never said so. But there again, she wouldn't have. She had all her things around her, few as they were. And looked at another way, this room of her own, this room to herself, must have been the triumph of her escape from childhood, where in the head groom's house on the estate there would have been inevitably a shared room for the five children. So that escape, that first position as a governess, would have been a marvellous one, that room to herself. The children she was governess to were still there, amongst the photographs on the chest of drawers. She still talked about them, about their achievements; the girl had married a doctor, the boy had gone to a public school and was now housemaster at another one. It sickened me. I knew their stories off by heart, so often was I told them. Now I can recall almost none of it.

When she was housekeeper to the local railway manager, again she had a room to herself. The manager was a genial old reactionary. He fulminated against Stalin, Archbishop Makairios, Aneurin Bevan. He enthused over Churchill, Beaverbrook, Anthony Eden. His daughter had married an Olympic runner who became headmaster of the grammar school to which I won a scholarship. Endlessly my aunt would talk about the grandchildren, my headmaster's children, what amazing children, what promise, what achievements, what beauty, what brilliance, until I began to hate them with an implacable loathing. That made no difference. They were always there. At every visit, from my teens to my fifties, I had to hear about them: and there was always, as with everything in her conversation, the implied rebuke, why are you not like these impeccable children, these are the models for you to emulate, this is the social ladder for you to climb, to be like them. But you couldn't as far as I could see. This was England. The classes were castes. The gulf between manual labourer' children and the public (i.e. private) school-educated offspring of the bourgeoisie was not to be bridged. I had no wish to acquire those strangulated accents. I had no wish to pretend to be other that what I was. What I was was hard enough to know. But to pretend to be something other, that would always be a pretence, always be detected. It was such a relief to get to Australia. And that, I suppose, was the final disgrace, the final mark of my not being like those splendid children. I had left England. I had deserted. In the First World

War they had shot people like that, like me. Some three hundred and seven of their own troops they executed in World War I.

When the railway manager died my aunt had to find somewhere to live. I think she was left some money. And perhaps she had saved a bit. My father tried to persuade her to buy a house, to provide herself with some security. But she wouldn't. Perhaps she could not accept the indignity of it: here was my father, a working man, a manual worker, giving advice on property. Perhaps she was afraid of the responsibility. Whatever, she missed the opportunity.

So it was a succession of rooms. I think the first place was a couple of rooms and a kitchen. But it is the sitting room that I remember, with the afternoon light coming in. It was at the corner of Sunnyside Road, and because of the name I remember it as a sunny room. Not that she liked the sun. She made a point of keeping out of it, wore hats that shaded her face, kept a pale complexion. I think it was a mark of refinement for her not to be sunburned. Whereas my mother, who loved to potter around the garden in all winds and weathers, would develop the dark, suntanned, wind burned complexion of a countrywoman, a gypsy even. But being a countrywoman was what my aunt was distancing herself from. It was a matter of separating herself from the soil, aiming for the alienation of privilege. So she would have had the lace curtains drawn across the window to filter out the intrusive light, and if the sun was shining in directly, she would have pulled the full, heavy curtains across too, to block it.

She had never married. She was the classic maiden aunt. Those were the years of that classic type. And I don't think it was with her, as perhaps it was with my father's two sisters, a matter of choice, a matter of preference. She was of the generation whose husbands who might have been were mown down in the First World War. The millions of them sacrificed to the nationalists, the arms-manufacturers, the politicians, the generals, the business interests. There was never any choice. Just a mass carnage that left a mass desolation, spinster aunts living in single rooms, sewing by the light of the window, but sewing not for children of their own but for nephews and nieces, writing letters in the fading light, but not to children of their own or their own absent partner. They were the unburied victims, the unslaughtered, the ones who survived to a life of incompletion, isolation, the loneliness of an independence they surely would never have chosen, if choice had been theirs.

'She hasn't had an easy life,' my mother would say. When she was housekeeper to the railway manager and his wife, when there were visitors, she always had to sit at the back of the room, on a hard chair, at the back of the room away from the fire, in that cold draughty house.

I could never quite visualise these occasions. Perhaps they were too painful. Perhaps the image told more of my mother's priorities. My mother loved to have a fire going, would sit beside it in her easy chair, prodding and poking away at it. 'Leave the damn fire alone,' my father would complain. The fire was my mother's delight, and to her those rooms my aunt lived in without open fireplaces were soulless, like their landladies who always at some point decided they needed the room for themselves or for a relative or they decided to sell up, and my aunt had to find somewhere else to move to.

Well, that happened twice: and every move is a major stress, a massive disruption. After the second time she moved to an old people's home with its self-contained units, its bed sitting room and kitchen. It was an indignity at first, of course, subsidised council accommodation, a provision of that socialist welfare state she so condemned and which is now being demolished. She kept herself in superior splendour, like most of the people there. 'That great big sitting room and no one uses it,' my mother would remark. The communal room was always empty. Everyone preferred to stay alone, each in his or her own cell, writing letters to absent relatives in the fading light, sewing beside the window, or looking out at the rooks nesting in the high cedars.

The last room was in the nursing room. The smallest room of all, only a few sticks of furniture remaining now, only the few that could be fitted in. Now she was in her nineties, no longer able to look after herself. There was the window, a few sparrows chirruping in the branches of a tree, the occasional sound of pigeons cooing. She could no longer manage to write letters, no longer maintain that determined connection with the family, with former charges, with friends. And indeed most of her correspondents had now died. She no longer bothered with television or radio. It was not just that she could not operate them. She was no longer interested. Slowly she was withdrawing from the constrictions of the world. She was back in conversation with her mother, she was living on some intermediate plane, wafting back in and out of the present to some other dimension.

The last time I saw her she asked, 'And where have you come from?'

'Sydney,' I said.

'Oh, really,' she said. 'How interesting. I have a nephew in Sydney.'

'That's me,' I said. 'I am your nephew.'

'Are you?' she said. 'Do you know him?'

The photographs still stood on the chest of drawers. Her older brother, one-time butler, in his army uniform. Her youngest brother in air-force uniform, standing beside a palm tree in Egypt. A family photograph of my parents, my sister and me of nearly fifty years back. The children she had been governess to. Lady Diana on horseback, standing there, yes, definitely static. And the mementoes, the carved elephant from Egypt her brother had brought from the Middle East, the carved goanna I had brought from Australia, little boxes, a clock no longer going.

'How did you get here?' she asked.

'I hired a car.'

'You hired a pony and trap?' she said.

I hear it pass down the narrow, hedged lane, the clip clop of the hooves echoing in the still night, as the white flash of a barn owl rises up out of an overhanging elm.

Thank You, Miss

As the bus hurtled down the hill towards us at the stop he said, stepping from beneath the shelter to the edge of the pavement, waiting momentarily in the drizzle before climbing the steps of the as yet unstationary vehicle, 'I've decided I'm not going to teach.' It was – after seventeen years of being taught and the last few of intending teaching, to depart from the covering cap and furling gown and leap, as it were, onto the stream of, so to speak – a decision. A shuddering of the clutch and a chugging away, past the detacheds with their long drives and hedged fronts and gables and a sevenpenny bus ride; the privilege of suburbia has it tax.

But it had always been easier to get onto a bus then, at those first two stops, in the mornings; it got you to school, while nearer in you often had to walk or miss communal prayers and atone with a fifty-minute detention which brought you successfully into the five o'clock bus-crowded rush hour on the way back home; though even starting the journey in suburbia meant having someone on your knees, bare in short trousers but short enough not to graze – the knees – on the back of the seat in front. Half fares crammed together, five in a double seat, to justify the half expenditure and save space and the push of standing. At a stop lower down – implying no less select a domestic residence – two or more masters would enter the already crowded bus – unless they were able to thumb, though without so direct an importunity, a lift from a wealthier head of a department or writer of text-books; and packed on the bus, glaring as well as a glare was possible without the symbolic pipe dropping from the gums, they would confront the fledgling sparrow-nested five who would shuffle and grovel and disentwine limbs and touch caps as hopeful placatory gestures. There was a man, a bull of a man with no ring in his heavy nostrils, no master but a nodding acquaintance of one – he clearly valued that permission to nod – who demanded often that the seats should be surrendered, and five with heads down and eyes looking up under their cap peaks, would sheepishly line out into the gangway to enable two old cows to sit; a nonsensical disposition of cargo, it always seemed, but obeyed from either the glaring master with a bullet hole through his chin from the First World War and eccentric since, or from his nodding acquaintance.

'It's not only that the pay's no good,' he said; 'the starting salary's all right but it's misleading; it goes up so slowly. It's I don't want to be stuck, labelled a schoolmaster...' They were quite pleasant houses, but on the main road and so nowhere near the best; they were noisy and smoky from traffic; and for him, now, the best only was good enough; it wasn't having tasted the milk of paradise and honey dew; but having seen people who had tasted it and clearly had thrived bonnily on it, that gave him a disinclination for forty odd years of thirds of a pint of school milk, and the jangle of first-formers carrying a crate between them round to the form rooms, and occasionally slipping and dropping one with a familiar echo down the concrete stairs. To be stuck here, chalky and underpaid; no, it wasn't even that; it was *here*, and the surety that everywhere else was here, a bus ride to a deserted town centre, sevenpence to the Cross.

The bus pulled out to pass a line of four or five cars, parked by old dears who were having a bridge party in one of the houses with a rather shorter drive now. A hitch-hiker thumbed, damp in the drizzle, outward bound traffic on the other side of the road.

'That's the point,' he said, 'no one knows; it's no good asking; who knows anything about business?' Just as boring. 'But there'll be more money to be bored with.' Spirits instead of bitter.

It wasn't the teaching; it was all that that symbolized, the years spent absorbing in the desert, and then a plunge back to the desert, beneath the inadequate parasol of the wind filled parachute, dragging along the sand the corpse of the shot down man, not a jackal to eat him, no indignant desert birds to wheel, preserved unputrescent by the dry heat.

The neck of the woman who had appeared in the seat in front was browned by the sun, or a cosmetic to simulate the rays. Indubitably attractive on a quite unsymbolic level, but the dried irrigation channels told of the passing of the years; suggested winged time even carrying her through the sands; but suggested too – something unascertainable – the tongued moisture of lovers. It was that sort of neck; but full many a flower is etc on the desert air etc. Certainly, if wasted, it had been a fragrant sweetness; the neck was held at just that fragrantial shedding angle, the hair clipped between the neat and the brazen – hard, metallic, gritty but irrigable. The summer dress disclosed just that little too much of the forty years old shoulder, beneath the shifting furrows the neck turned too surely.

'Oh God, as long as I don't have to stick somewhere like this.' Terracing had now developed, the town was closing in, with the blank brick walks shading who-knew-what lock-up garages. Posters proclaimed YOUNG CONSERVATIVES NEED YOU alongside the week's film programme; TAKE OFF YOUR CLOTHES AND LIVE, or the passionate lusts of CALL GIRL. But the chemist's window showed only nappies and baby scales, no contraceptives. It was a nice town to live in. So are they all, nice towns.

The woman in front got up and moved across the gangway. This fidgeting, as she before had been fidgeting in her handbag, spoke more of neurosis than the bed; in a nice town perhaps the only possibility. She looked around and smiled; from the teeth at the front she looked older, was older. The speculations were possible, the irrigations less likely to have been carried out; it's expensive work taking all that equipment so far; and now with the Bomb testing there, the danger of fall-out has arisen with possible genetic damage.

'Hello,' he smiled back.

'How are you getting *on*?' She gabbled four words to croon on the *on*.

'Oh,' he shrugged, 'you know,' with his hands disclaiming responsibility, 'so so.'

'You've finished now?' she called, across the gangway.

'Yes.'

'What are you going to *do*?'

Resting prone on the *do* she made it sound easy.

'I don't know,' he said, 'but I've decided not to teach.'

'Have you now?' she said. 'I thought you would, you know. Yes, I did' – lovingly, caressingly, as if he had contradicted. 'It wasn't for you? You want something larger, something with wider horizons. Yes, if I know you, wider horizons, that's what you want.'

She leaned forward across the gangway but the neck of her dress was too tight to look down to her breasts.

'I'm sure you'll do well.'

There were other passengers on the bus.

'Oh well, oh, well, oh, well, thank you.'

'No, I mean it,' and lest we forget, reiterated, 'wider horizons.'

The lone and level sands stretch far away.

'So what are you going to *do*?'

'Ah, well, I don't know.'

'Now my nephew,' the way she moved her head she should have had ear-rings, large and jangling; 'my nephew, now, he wanted to teach.'

She stood up, another sudden movement, and came to the seat behind.

'The draft,' indicating an open ventilation window, suggesting this caused her continual motion, whether to avoid disarray to her hair or arthritis to her shoulder. She leant her elbow on the chromium top of the seat back, its point reaching between us, putting her head forward to cause an embarrassment of proximity of bare arm and quick glancing eye, of offered brown lusts in a public place, and the ever waiting slap of a schoolmistress's hand and back rigid with denial and accusation.

'He wanted to go into teaching after he'd been in the army but he had to pass some more exams which was just nonsense but anyway they said he'd have to and I said to him do you really want to don't let your mum and dad push you into it do you want to end up like your aunt so he went into engineering and got married with a child and then started up on his own and now he's got the contract for rebuilding the education offices and a lovely house with twenty-eight acres of ground and two cars one for his wife and twenty men under him and he's gone off for holiday to the south of France. There.'

She prodded him with a finger and me, simultaneously, with the elbow. A success story. The bus juddered away from traffic lights and passed the park; the swings and slides were deserted in the drizzle; the trees flourished, planted as a living memorial for the slaughter of Gheluvelt. The site of some old cottages had been cleared and covered with used cars. This week's bargain was a Vauxhall. An invitation was open to everyone to look round. The Co-op offered slashing reductions. So did a supermarket opposite.

'And now,' she said, beadily, 'can I ask the name of your friend?'

There were another three stops before the first drink. Biography had to be advanced, participation, somehow, to be avoided. She was a person who made people feel at home. It was, one felt, a speciality of hers, this reassurance and polite enquiry, the settling in and the gossip. No child need ever go unscathed who came new to her class. His brothers sisters fathers mothers uncles, all would be elicited in the croon of her bosom. His first day would not be in the wilderness, but the curiosity of the zoo with the wild beasts staring enquiry over the rails. She would know the road he lived in with its social placing, drag from the child his father's occupation or profession, titles or professional qualifications, mother's maiden name, and two referees. Beaming the while. And offering in return generously her nieces and nephews, to be digested whole or sectionally; she was a trader, not a ravisher. She could be envisaged too, and he could be seen, too, envisaging her, in the staff room, exchanging marital infidelities for driving offences, bitching over the coffee fund and inclining, at that fragrantial angle, her head to the Head, plucking at her bra straps as he came to enquire about her form's progress and puckering, then, her lip, as if to say, *oh* – dwelling on the *oh* – I shouldn't be doing that in front of you – and fondling the you silkily in both hands – should I? While the mascara would flick up and down over the beadily ambiguous eyes, like the thirteen-year-olds flirting over the boiled cabbage in the canteen. What rather mattered was whether the dear lady was unique, whether her spinsterly fecundity was an isolated oasis, or whether a whole harem of such squatted there, had stripped the shading leaves from the palms, and fanned themselves with the fronds or inadequately clad their pudenda with the serrated foliage; worse, were they all touched by the sun, gossiping madly to each other to create an illusion of that white walled township, were they all intimately discussing drafts they had avoided, did they all have nephews who had made the big money? He seemed less disturbed by the intriguing irrigation channels than by the aridity of the air, with the insistent sameness of her all day and TAKE OFF YOUR CLOTHES AND LIVE at night. His shedding himself over the earth for wider horizons was hardly the point; the case was not of spreading out but building up. YOU CAN HIRE THIS BUS FOR PRIVATE PARTIES. PHONE A BRANCH OFFICE FOR DETAILS. Two old ladies disappeared into a pub for their evening stout. A policeman communicated with headquarters by radio-telephone on his motor bike. A couple of teddy-boys stood outside a car showroom window, one combing is hair and looking at his reflection. A crocodile of heavy legged girls waddled back from school to the dormitories, fee-paid and elocuted and comparatively spotless. Do they get free milk too? A tramp blew his nose with his fingers, snot dropping downward with a tenuous spider's thread, and falling suddenly in a glob to the gutter. The drizzle washed it away, after all. She elicited fragmentary biography.

And now, looking straight at her, over a shoulder (mine) at hers, behind, looking her, so to speak, in the mouth, she seemed less of a gift and you felt inclined to tell her age by her teeth. The eyes, the photographer's glance revealed, showed to better advantage against the dark of the blackboard than the linen sheet. It might have been, that croon, oh save us, maternal; or aunt-like, in the sense of one has too many aunts, not cognate with uncles. The twitches and movements, change of seat and fumbling of handbag – again she ferreted through it – were material for the wit of the playground, not the pleasantries of the saloon bar. 'Ah, here we are.' She held a penny at its edge, proffering our Queen's head like an identity disc to gain admission to a women's latrine. 'Would your kind friend do something for me?'

The wayside pulpit outside the Methodist chapel gave its comfort for the week. DON'T MAGIFY YOUR TROUBLES. GOD KNOWS THEY'RE BIG ENOUGH ALREADY. 'I've paid the wrong money. I thought I was getting off at the Cross but I meant to ask for the cathedral. Could you go up to the conductor boy and ask him to give me another penny ticket or change this one, there's a dear. He's down at the front, look.' The school mistress dominant, no sovereign lady offering a penny. The Queen's shilling and the Foreign Legion.

I was too tall for these games. Down the front indeed I could see him, young and bad-tempered and how was he to know I dissociated myself from the idiocy; she was near and acute enough to hear any dissociation. A wry face.

The observer erect, reluctantly participant. To die for his lady. Fuck, he says to himself, no longer equivocal or relishing of ambiguities. The bus pulled into the penultimate stop, no good pretending to leave here, oh, if only later, and a sorry but I must run into the welcoming arms of the buxom barmaid, clasp my lolling tongue to her bosom and buy three light ales. Never before had the tavernal gloom seemed more desirable. Oh, Horn and Trumpet deliciously stammered, the freeing of burden on the Pack Horse and bare backed bucking through the waves most Antony-like at the Dolphin, real, all, oh real. The Charles' Head and the Swan with Two Nicks, the Five Ways and the bardic Shakespeare, the Hop Market and the Vaults, the Shades, the Duke of Wellington, the Talbots Old and New, the Green Man, the Five Feathers, the Saracen's Head and the Coventry Arms, the Gardener's Arms, the Carpenter's Arms, the Farrier's Arms, the barmaid's white and welcoming arms and hands soft calloused from the black beer pumps.

PASSENGERS ARE REQUIRED BY LAW TO STATE THEIR DESTINATION CLEARLY AND TENDER THE CORRECT FARE. The observer observed the stencilled signs no more, but drew into a seat; a potential passenger stepped uncertainly inwards, unwilling to clash in the narrow gangway. The young boy glared 'Are you coming or going?' Delay and thought; staying. The passenger settled, our hero advances with deliberation, conscious of Miss watching. Please Miss can I leave the.

Careful by subtle sentencing and intonation of equivocal phrase to dissociate and suggest intimacy of attitude of smiling toleration.

'Excuse me, the lady back here wants another penny ticket, she's going further or something.'

'Well, the lady better' he said, mumbling or implying. I gave him her penny and present ticket, pressed them clammily into his palm, and turned to walk back to her. The conductor followed and walked past to the back of the bus.

'What did he say?'

Guiltily inadequate. 'I don't know, I didn't hear. He's going to' and mumble and implication.

She stopped him on his return.

'Well it's twopence more.'

'It is not.'

'It is, madam.'

The title deliberately affronted the fragrantial blossom; he spat on her pollen.

'Let me tell you it isn't. Look in your little book. And if an inspector comes, ask him. I know.'

Decelerating, the bus pulled in to the Cross.

'Bye,' we smiled, leaving her for her whist drive in the cathedral shadow, and as we left the steps the poker faced inspector prepared to ascend. It was still drizzling, just as wetly; that it seemed less of an irritation was a pleasant but subjective delusion.

Don't Go Having Kittens

I remember that time travelling down on the Cathedrals Express in the middle of winter, my hands freezing as I tried to clear the windows of condensation to look at the white, still countryside. No heating was on. I'd sat as long as I could, hunched into my coat, the door of the compartment continually being opened and shut by people walking along the corridor and looking in, hoping for a warmer carriage, and then I heard a voice say it would be warmer nearer the engine. So I followed out into the corridor, pushing my way through people going in each direction, standing stamping their feet, curling their palms hopefully round cigarettes.

It must have been the last but one carriage that turned out not to be for passengers at all. I'd pushed open the door out of the shaking, rattling platform, stood there swaying on what felt no securer than Sweeney Todd's trapdoor, as the flexible sides creased and buckled like a concertina, and I moved uncertainly, unbalanced – the Cathedrals travelled very fast on some stretches – to open the door into the next carriage. The connecting platform was like some pressurisation chamber by which to enter one spaceship from another, or the valve of a huge mechanical heart. Pumped through like cold reptilian blood I stood in the corridor not of a passenger carriage but a wire-partitioned parcels van, carrying nothing but two coffins, each draped and bound in black hessian to protect their polished wood.

I looked out of the window at the cold steel rails and frozen gravel bed, lurching with the swaying of the train's speed, refrigerated with the two bodies, rattling and hurtling through a cold countryside whose only signs of life were imprints on the snow of crows' and starlings' feet.

A couple of hours separated the Midland corpses from my arrival. I left the train at Paddington and walked to the ticket barrier beside the trough of hissing steam clouding over the platform, shooting from beneath the engine and through the stationary wheels to rise to the high overarching roof. Girders vaulted this final nave, swooping like the tracks of a big dipper, bowing into cupolas, great convexities gathering the rising steam. The ironwork was pierced with bolt holes, slits and huge circles so that it stretched overhead in gentle curves of black lace, silhouetted against the light outside. While closer, the pillars could be seen more clearly, bracing and angling firm girders, nuggetty with hexagonal boltheads, black from protective paint and the settling powder of soot. Banners could have been hung down, flags captured from defeated armies, tapestries cloaking the walls; but neat posters and timetables and magazines on bookstalls provided the only colour. And hunched taxi drivers in black cabs with darkened windows were the only muffled coachmen for unknown destinations. Light seeped in through the great domes and arches, penetrating the fallen grime as softly as snow or settling pigeons, and the air became clearer as the steam dropped and the boilers of the engine cooled beside the platforms sheathing its long length.

The first thing we did was get a drink. There was a little dark pub near where Lydia worked and we dropped in there. She asked me about a few people, people who'd introduced me to her; we hardly knew each other, no more than an hour's necking on the river bank by the cathedral after the pub shut, and two or three beery evenings when we'd all been drinking together. But I'd said I'd look her up when I was in London and it seemed worth making the effort.

Though her mother was discouraging. We went back to the flat because she wanted to change from the clothes she'd been working in. As her mother was home we decided – or Lydia decided – to wander around the embankment till the pubs opened again and kill time in them till we went to a party I'd been invited to. I sat in the living room while she changed, perched on the edge of a couch.

'You're going out, are you?' her mother asked.

'Just have a wander round,' I said.

'You might as well. No point in staying here. Though it'll be just as much a bleeding waste of time.'

There was the sound of Lydia moving a chair or shutting a wardrobe door.

'You won't get anywhere with her,' her mother said, 'wasting your bloody time.'

I nodded, smiling, sociable.

'Must be bleeding daft,' said her mother, short, fattening, her hair not recently combed, her make-up not put on. She went back into the kitchen.

'Do you want a drink?' she asked.

'No thanks, it's all right, we've just had one.'

'Please yourself,' she said tersely. 'If you don't want nothing you won't be disappointed when you don't get it.'

I sat, looking at the brown wallpaper, the table cluttered with magazines and newspapers, glass fruit bowls filled with hair pins and cotton bobbins.

'Tarted yourself up, ain't you,' she said when Lydia appeared.

'Not specially,' Lydia said, 'though I could think of worse ways of looking.'

Her mother cackled instead of getting annoyed as I'd thought she would, cackled and put her hand up to the back of her head as if to make sure her coiffure was as it should be, that was the gesture, and scratched her scalp. She said. 'There's no point in dressing the bird if you ain't going to stuff it.'

Lydia seemed to snort and say something, though without opening her lips.

'Don't go having kittens,' her mother said. And before Lydia could speak she'd added, 'One day you'll realize what you've been missing and it'll be too late to have any.'

'Ready?' Lydia asked me.

'Ready hours ago I should reckon,' her mother said, 'and probably withered away to nothing now. Needs to pull his bloody socks up. Just wasting your bleeding time,' she assured me again. 'Tight as a bloody wall plug she is. It's no bloody use thinking you'll get anywhere. Still,' she conceded, 'it's your choice. I'd pull my socks up if I was you though; else you'll never pull them pants down.' And she laughed herself into a coughing fit, her cheeks bulging red, as Lydia banged shut the door.

It wasn't so cold in London. The snow hadn't got that far south. So except for the wind nipping our noses and ears it was pleasant walking along the embankment, catching glimpses of tall chimneys and high spires beneath the black arched bridges, skylines of domes and towers as you looked along the river. But we hadn't much to say. I watched her as we walked, looking at her legs in dark green stockings as she stepped ahead of me, at cheeks touched light red by the wind as she turned round to speak, at the lines of her breasts as she leant over the balustrade of a bridge; and occasionally we would bump against each other, jostled by other pedestrians. But it wasn't until we had spent the early evening drinking and were leaving the party to go on to another one someone had heard of that my hand went round her through the night, resting softly beside her breast, and she put her hand for warmth into the pocket of my coat and like dragons our breath was puffs of white condensation in the cold.

We were both pretty pissed when we got back to the flat and so was Lydia's mother. I don't know where she'd been but we'd been drinking a quarter bottle of whisky on a deserted tube station for what had seemed hours. It was too late to catch my train home.

'You can sleep at our place anyway,' Lydia said. So we went back for that, lurching through the mysteries of London, slavering steam.

'He's gone,' her mother said, standing in the doorway to the living room, her hair more in need of combing, her cheeks sagging, the sides of her mouth drooping, no longer supported and protruded by teeth.

'He'll come back,' Lydia said, her bottom neat and firm as she walked in front of me down the hall.

'No, he's gone, gone right out for good this time.' She let go of the one door jamb, gripping with her finger tips pressed white to the other and swinging round as if by some lateral gravity to let us through to the room.

'Sodded right off.'

A lampshade lay shattered on the floor, its covering ripped away, its frame bent. There was a glass broken, too. Lydia went out to the kitchen and drank some water from the tap. She came back in, wiping her mouth and chin with her hand, and started clearing up the wreckage.

'Sit down,' her mother told me. 'Have a drink. Have something to eat, I bet you've not eaten, what do you want?'

'I'm not really hungry,' I said.

'Course you are, what you need's a nice piece of fish. Lydia,' she yelled.

'I can hear.'

'Well bloody well jump to then. Get the fish out of the fridge.'

'I'm not really hungry,' I said.

'He doesn't want anything,' Lydia began.

'Of course he does but he doesn't know what he's missing. You don't know what's good for you,' she said.

'Honestly, I'm not really –'

'You don't want my fish, is that it, you're turning up your running nose at it, getting all high and mighty is that it, snooked up little cock…'

She stopped for breath and the reassembly of her forces, then drew herself up, raising her chin into her palate and upper lip, closing her eyes for concentration.

'I cook fish amongst the best in the whole metropolis. No fish comes out of my oven that isn't done to a treat, treated to a turn, as soft and tender and juicy as could be wished for. Do you think I can't cook at my age, is that it? I'm not as old as I look, not with my teeth in…'

'It's not that…'

'Too proud to eat it, just because I've lost my dentures. Lydia,' she called, as if to ask her to find them. 'I'm good enough to breed that bloody tart you can take gallivanting off, but not to cook fish.'

Lydia grimaced at me.

'And there's no good your pulling faces you bloody cast-iron virgin,' she said. 'You let him just make up his own mind for once. Show him somebody in this bleeding house's generous enough to give him something without him having to batter through a bloody brick wall to get at it.'

'Well, just a small bit,' I conceded.

'Course you will, it's no trouble, and it's cooked beautiful the way I do it. Now just sit down' – she cleared the couch of newspapers with one swing of her arm – 'and it'll be only two shakes of a lamb's tail.'

We all sat as I ate the fish, Lydia watching me like a starving cat.

'There's none left so you can't have any,' her mother said. 'And don't you,' she said, glaring at me over the creases of her eyes, 'go giving her any. I cooked it for you and it's you as'll eat it. She gets fed enough.'

I chewed alone.

'He just went off,' said her mother, 'off into the cold black night. The lousy bastard.'

It seemed a long time before her mother at last went off to bed. And when she did go, she told Lydia to go too.

'I'm going to help him make up the couch,' Lydia said.

'That's a bloody waste of time, too,' her mother said.

'He's got to sleep somewhere.'

'There's enough empty beds in the house, enough bloody half-empty ones, anyhow; there's no need to go making any more.'

I licked the taste of fish round my teeth.

'You don't need,' her mother went on, 'a whole bloody double bed to yourself.'

'I'm making up the couch,' Lydia said with dignity. She might have said, 'Nor do you', but thank God she didn't.

Her mother swayed at the doorway. 'When you've bloody had it you won't be so bloody eager to throw it away,' she said, and left. And after she had come back to say goodnight to us both, and lament tearfully on his departure, the room was left to us alone.

'He's probably in a cell,' Lydia said. 'Last time he went off he bit a police dog and got locked up for the night. He'll come back.'

She insisted on making up the couch. Not immediately. We lay on it for a while and kissed, but when I tried to stroke her breasts she stopped me. So we lay there together, parallel, almost asleep, the alcohol swirling the steam through our heads and veins.

'We might as well both sleep here,' I said.

'It's too uncomfortable.'

'Well,' I said, edging my fingers beneath her bra, 'your double bed would be comfortable.'

'It would be,' she said, 'but it's not going to be.' And she sat up, grazing my knuckles as the edge of her bra sliced across them when she moved away.

She made up the couch for me and went off to her bedroom to sleep. Either she drank less or could take more than her mother.

I was woken by a noise in the corridor, perhaps a door banging though I could not be sure. I lay awake, listening. Then footsteps padded along. I could not tell if they were coming towards the door of the living room or going away from it. I lay still, holding my breath, trying to catch the fragments of sounds. A moaning sent my body rigid, a howl of despair. I waited, the silence and waiting worse than the cry itself. In the tunnel that led from the cathedral to the nunnery, one of the poor novitiates had once got lost, and found too late, her cold, virgin form rigid in death. She still walked the tunnel terrifying the youngest boarders in the school on the nunnery site with her helpless, directionless footsteps, her deep wordless cries. It came again. I dared not move, cowered from intruding on this unknown presence. It was hardly human, that inexplicable, brief howl. And then it gave voice, cried 'Oh God, oh my God,' and the possessive seemed to screw tighter the anguish.

The padding footsteps wandered aimlessly up and down the corridor, stopping, starting, turning, so that no sustained movement was being made, it was not a pacing from one end to the other.

'Oh God, oh it's terrible, oh God, oh my God, what can I do?' The words tailed off into sobs.

'And the night he's gone off too, oh God, why does it have to be when he goes off? The lousy stinking bastard, why did he have to go and go?'

I felt sick at whatever nameless terror had provoked this.

'Oh God,' she called, 'oh God fuck him. And fuck the bleeding cat. Oh why's it have to happen?'

The voice fell silent for a while and then, agonised from her room, cried out again, 'It's hideous, I can't bear it. I shall be sick, oh the poor little bastards.' And then more clearly, standing again in the corridor, she called out, 'Lydia, Lydia, quick, wake up, it's terrible, Lydia.'

There was no answer.

'Wake up, why don't you wake up, Lydia.'

I lay rigid in terror, seeing Lydia's ravaged, crushed in body sprawled on the floor. But Lydia called from her bed, 'What is it?'

'Don't ask what is it, come on here, quick. And the night he's gone and walked out, too.'

'He'll be back,' said Lydia, briefly, curtly.

'It's the cat,' she cried, 'it's the cat, it's gone and had kittens. And it's never had them for six years and it has to go and choose tonight to have them and oh, they're awful.'

'They'll be all right,' said Lydia. 'Go back to bed. I've got to go to work in the morning.' Her voice was muffled, resentful, beneath blankets.

'But they're awful, they're all terrible, they're all – oh God, I can't bear it the poor little bastards, Lydia, oh –'

Above the sobbing I heard Lydia walk across her room. There was the faint click of a door lock. Then the footsteps across the room again.

'Christ, Lydia,' she called, 'are you bleeding getting up?' And suddenly impatient she ran down the corridor and grabbed at the door handle to burst into Lydia's room.

'Oh you lousy bitch, you street walking dirty little tart,' she cried, and beat at the locked door with her fists, hammering and pounding on the wood that frustrated all her efforts.

'You little bitch, come and help me. The cat's gone and had kittens and he's not here to do anything and oh God, it's terrible, oh they're all joined together.'

My stomach suddenly heaved with a retching terror and I tasted, but somehow held down, the fish.

I pulled the blankets up tighter round me on the couch, hoping not to be involved in this domestic dispute, trying not to think of the monstrous birth. I had heard of animals strangled by the umbilical cord and wondered if one cord had strangled all the brood. Would they all have been fed from the one, peas suspended on a slender stem? Or were they truly more impossibly joined together, their backs knit in one multipedicellate growth?

She wept softly in the corridor, for the loss of her husband and daughter, and for that nocturnal visitation. And then she called out, clearly, suddenly, as with a new realization, 'You.'

I lay still in the darkness, for how could I know that it was me that she called?

'Hey, you.'

The night outside was silent.

'Hey you, you in there what's your name, you've got to help me. I can't bear it. I can't bear to look at them, they're so horrible, oh do something.'

Lydia said nothing. I hoped she would help me, call to her mother to leave me alone, get up herself. But she called out nothing at all, secure behind her locked door.

'Are you awake?'

And at that loud insistence I groaned as if roused, asking uncertainly, 'What?'

'Oh hurry,' she said, as if recording yet disregarding my dissimulation. 'You've got to help me. That lousy bitch has locked the door and the cat's gone and had kittens and oh –'

I tried to block my ears with the pillow and blankets to avoid the horror.

I switched on the standard light by the couch when she came in, fumbling through the door, a loose dressing gown wrapped round her which she clasped with one hand. She seemed to have been crying, her face reddened and blotchy. I blinked in the sudden light. She sat down on a cushion that was beside the couch, bending over to back down onto it, mounds of bosom bulging towards me, and, as suddenly, she was gone, her legs flung wide in an arc through the air as she tipped backwards. She disregarded that, sat down a second time with more deliberation, and straddled out her bare feet for balance.

'You've got to do something,' she said, 'the poor little bastards. I can't bear to look at them.'

At least I had no vision of them haunting me.

'What's your name?' she said. 'Why don't you get up? Somebody's got to do something.'

'Yes,' I said.

She leaned forward, moving it seemed to rest a hand on my knee, but I was beneath the blankets, not sitting on the couch.

'I won't hurt you, love,' she said, as I flinched when she nearly fell again.

'No,' I said.

All this time that agglutinous mass throbbed somewhere.

'You will help me, won't you?' she said.

She left me so I could dress. 'I'll just put some clothes on,' I suggested, as vest and underpants seemed unsuitable for the evening's work, and cold, too.

'Whatever you like,' she said, magnanimously.

I pulled on my trousers quickly, my head swinging black and aching with standing upright, my mouth dry and stale with the whisky and beer we had spent the evening drinking. While I pulled my shirt over my head I could hear her at Lydia's door, wheedling and begging help, shouting obscenities at the blocked keyhole. Then she came back.

She wouldn't let me see the kittens.

'Oh no, don't look, you mustn't look, it's horrible.'

My stomach reeled each time she said that. The shapeless vision of that pulsing abnormality clung to the fringes of my consciousness like some foul black squid. I didn't want to see them, didn't know what could be done.

'But you must do something,' she said. 'You can't leave the poor little buggers all like that.' And she began to sob, great heaving sobs, her hands pressed against her face.

'What do you want me to do, though?' I asked, insisting on my unwillingness.

She sobbed awhile, and then she said, taking a deep breath from her sobbing, 'The RSPCA.'

'But they won't be around at this time of night.'

'They will,' she said in a sob of faith.

'But what time is it?'

'I don't know, but they'll be there. They're always there,' she said, suddenly weeping, 'to help.'

'Do you want to phone them?' I asked.

'No,' she said, 'no, you phone them, I can't, I can't bear to.'

In the disordered flat with papers and biscuit tins flung around the room in the fight she had had with him, I could find no phone directory.

'I can't,' I said, 'I don't know the number.'

She stopped weeping, took her hands from her face on which their imprint remained in great red rashes, and looked amongst the mess of the room. I hoped that she wouldn't find it, hoped that Lydia would get up, hoped that the kittens would experience a late mitosis and leave. But I hoped with a faithless desperation.

She sat on the bed's edge while I phoned, a blotched leg disclosed by the dressing gown hanging open to her knee. The gown was buttonless and the belt trailed behind her so she sat holding it to her waist. It plunged, though, at the neck so that her breasts rose with each sob like surfacing octopuses. There was no answer from the RSPCA, just the steady purr of the number being called. If a horse had been in labour and needed a Caesarean, who would have helped?

We looked across the room at each other, the standard lamp throwing the only light. I couldn't go back to bed because she sat on it. And my conscience insisted that these more than Siamese kittens had to be coped with, buried in their polyhedral coffin, and first done to death. Unless some surgeon should separate them. Yet who would do that dividing, who would take them away as if they had never been, clear up that growth and multiparous afterbirth? They could not be left to suffer through the night. We sat in the silent room, the two of us in that whole quiet city that sent no sound from road or bordering flats; and there was not even the polyphonic wailing from an adjoining room.

'If the RSPCA aren't there,' I said, 'I don't know what we can do'

'Nor do I,' she said, her face crumpled and aghast.

'Maybe if you just went back to bed,' I said, 'we could get someone in the morning.'

I felt cowardly, dishonest, guilty.

'Oh God, no,' she said, 'never, not with all them under the bed.'

If the lamp had been a candle it would have guttered.

'You'll have to phone the police,' she said.

The voice of the constable who answered the phone projected an image of Edwardian protection, rich moustaches tinged blue by hissing gas lamps, felons with red scarves knotted round their ragged collars being brought cowering to the cells by officers whose spiked and chained helmets glistened as they passed.

'Just a minute,' he said, when I had outlined our problem, 'I think you'd best speak to the duty officer, sir.'

Though considerate, the duty officer was hardly helpful.

'Look,' I said to explain, 'it isn't my cat that's had the kittens. I don't live here. I don't even have a cat. I'm just phoning up for someone. I'm a sort of friend. It's nothing to do with me really.'

'I appreciate that sir,' he said, 'but it's not really anything to do with us. Doesn't come within our province. Why don't you try the RSPCA?'

'I have,' I said' 'there's no one there.'

'Oh,' he said, 'that's unusual; you'll just have to leave it till they open in the morning then.'

'I suppose so,' I said, slowly, pleasingly.

'I'll tell you what,' he said, relenting into generosity.

'Yes?'

'I'll tell you what.' He stopped again momentarily and then added, 'Have you got a strong stomach?'

'Oh, you must do something,' she wailed from the bed.

'Yes,' I said, uncertainly, tentatively.

'What you want to do,' he said, 'is get a bucket – you with me? Good – get a bucket, a good large one, fill it with water – you with me? – and put them in it. It's quick and it'll be over with. All right, sir?'

'All right,' I said.

The hall in the flat was ill lit, a dull light bulb dropping a yellow haze over the brown, smudgy walls. It hadn't been papered or painted for years, and no light came from open doors to dispel the gloom. Footsteps in it didn't echo but felt cold and clammy, feet touching the floor with such a lack of resonance that the sudden cessation of sound at each movement was more disturbing than any creaking floorboard or squeaking door. She followed behind me as if for protection. From Lydia's room came the steady rise and fall of breathing. But there were no other sounds. We might have been creeping along some subterranean tunnel, slowly to suffocate.

The bucket was in the lavatory at the end of the hall, beneath a cracked, grey, basin. At least I knew where the lavatory was to vomit, now. And the bucket was nauseous enough, lined with a grey, furry scum, old dry rags or mop heads inside.

'The tap doesn't work,' she said.

I decided to leave the bucket for the moment, defer the grim task of filling that, and locate the ball of kittens.

'But they're too horrible,' she said again, grabbing with both her hands at me and then releasing her hold to wrap her dressing gown back to her.

'I shall have to see them sooner or later,' I said.

And with that we set off back down the corridor, my stomach a tight ball bouncing and clutching uncertainly, my cheeks burning from the cold of the day and the alcohol and the phone calls.

'Stop,' she said, resting one hand on the door jamb of her bedroom, then slowly opening the door. She beckoned at me with her head, her eyes floating askew, her tongue, out in anticipation, lolling loose.

'Under there,' she said.

Standing, I couldn't see; so we both knelt down on the carpet, her breasts hanging like udders as she bent over to lift the hem of a blanket that had dropped over the bed's edge.

I looked slowly, cautiously, at the dust, at two empty gin bottles, at a brandy bottle, at a black, coagulate mass.

'That –.'

'There it is,' she whispered, 'there they are.'

Her eyes shone at the rediscovery.

I looked more carefully, steadying my focus.

'It's not –,' I began.

'Do you think I don't know, do you think I'm just imagining?' she said, with a sudden venom, furious at my doubts. 'Do you think I'd go and imagine something like that, something as horrible as that?' And reminded of the horror she sobbed again.

'No, I can't see properly,' I said. 'How do we get another light on?'

'Over there, by the bed.'

I skirted well clear of the bed lest some clammy tendril should grope out at me.

'That?' I said, as we looked again.

She nodded, and I looked more closely, still unsure, trying to discard the mental vision to see the object more clearly. I still shared her moments of pulsing terror. I reached beneath the bed gingerly, cautiously, like probing at an inflated corpse with a barge pole. The tips of my fingers gripped on to the shape and as I brought it nearer from under the bed I pulled with an increasing conviction, terror flowing from my arm and dispersing into the high shades of night.

'It's not kittens,' I said, 'it's –,' and rather than enunciate to her then in that bed and robed proximity, held out to her, almost as a suggestion, a black bra.

'Well,' she said, her eyes wide with surprise, a hand on my bended knee, 'well, would you ever believe it?'

I shook my head.

Lydia woke me the next morning, not with a hand on my bare shoulder or even with a cup of tea, but by drawing the curtains open to show the harsh, steel fog. I took the bus into the city with her because I didn't know the way alone, and we left her mother sleeping deeply and undisturbed back in the flat.

There was time for a coffee, insulated by a steamed-over plate-glass window from the crowds on the pavements, before she had to be at work. I looked at her across the table, her cheeks fresh with the cold, her eyes still gummed from sleep as if she were just looking over the sheets and not half awake.

'Those kittens,' I said, and she smiled as I mentioned them.

My leg touched her beneath the table and I pushed it against her knees which she held close, resistant, her dark winter stockings rasping against the fabric of my trousers.

'Oh,' she said, and she yawned, she really wasn't awake, 'it happens every time. We've not even had the cat for seven years.'

She pulled her legs away from my knee and tucked them behind the iron frame of her chair.

Like Rat Turds to Me

When Bob and Helen moved into the house, Helen probably said something like, 'How terrible to have such a big house for only two people.' She would have meant nothing by it, would have felt no unease that in the village there were seven children to a bedroom, and here there were seven bedrooms to each of them, or something almost as ridiculous. She would have meant nothing by it except how wonderful it is to have a huge house; just as her father had used to say how terrible it was that his Jaguar did only twelve miles to the gallon. And at the same time she would have smiled secretly and knowingly to herself – something she had done even before she was pregnant – that soon there would not just be the two of them.

Bob rather shambled. He was tall and quite broad-shouldered, but he would lower his head slightly as he walked, and his hair was repeatedly matted and ruffled. He was always running his hands through it in perplexity at some problem – at where to drink next, at how to explain a smashed rear light, at how to bandage a cut leg after falling over a concrete mixer outside a pub. The problem now was how to paint the house, with all its rooms, all grubby.

The house should have been in large grounds, approached by an avenue, fronted by smooth-shaven lawn; and a ha-ha wall should have allowed from the wide windows of the drawing room an unrestricted view of spreading oak-shaded meadows. It was a large, symmetrically-fronted Georgian house, three storeys and attics, with a fine white pediment that had become mossed and pitted and blackened, and finely proportioned windows from whose frames the paint had peeled. And it stood in an untidy village, nor far from the town, surrounded by piled-up cottages and hen-pens and service stations and bus shelters and road signs. Bushes did not hide it from the road; and at the back creeping cottages hemmed it in.

And so they had bought it cheaply, because of all this and its poor condition. It was really the only way in which they could have got such a house. They had not long been married, and Bob hadn't saved much. And her father was unwilling to keep lending them money to pay for Bob's crashed cars. It was unfair that she had to suffer this financial deprivation through Bob's idiocies.

She couldn't bear to move into the house as it was, so while they were still at the flat, Bob cleaned out the bedroom, the one that was to be theirs, prepared the walls with sugar-soap, washed them down, and painted them. It took the weekend. When he got down to things Bob was amazingly efficient. At the same time Helen, who couldn't do much because of being pregnant, cleaned up the kitchen the plumber had already re-equipped, and Bob in the evenings of the week painted that a clean new white. They would live in the kitchen, cook and eat there, while Bob got the rest of the house ready.

She was pleased at how quickly things were being done; and pleased, as she sat in the kitchen conceiving details of antique furniture that she would acquire, that Bob was painting the walls and not spending all his time drinking in town. Although she did not mind his drinking; when they had first met they had gone out a lot drinking, around the country pubs that their friends used to go to. But now he seemed less inclined to go out to those places, more to drink in town with Colin and Bill and John, who he'd bring back when the pubs shut. There was the awful time when Colin trampled in to see them, at the flat which it was so good no longer to be living in, wearing his army boots and trampling mud and rain all up the stairs, on the carpet, and studding holes into the linoleum with the hob nails. It was only an affectation to wear those boots; and even if he couldn't afford anything else, he could always get a job and earn some money. But Colin preferred to draw the dole and sit in the pub.

After the week's dutiful painting, Bob had earned a Saturday night's drinking he felt. Pregnant, she shouldn't drink; pregnant, she would have to sit alone in the empty house.

'I don't see that you have to, but if that's the way you feel…' said Bob.

She was in bed by the time Bob got home, having gone on for coffee with Colin and Bill and John and the rest, who didn't like an evening to break up, and always hoped to chat up some bird at one of the coffee bars. She wasn't really sleeping when he came back, and she couldn't decide whether to pretend to be asleep and not speak, or to claim that he had woken her. But Bob must have assumed her wakefulness since, as he dragged his shirt over his head, ruffling up his hair that he had tried to flatten down, he expounded his scheme immediately.

Colin had nowhere to live; he had had to leave his digs, and then the girl he had been sleeping with had got tired of his sleeping with her every night, and booted him out. And as there was so much painting to do, far more than Bob could manage in the evenings and at weekends, he'd agreed with Colin that it would be to everyone's advantage and convenience if Colin were to move in. He wouldn't have to pay anything, but he could help paint the house during the week, and do his own painting – he painted – in one of the many rooms.

'But why, Bob?' Helen asked.

'Because he's got nowhere to live and because we've got to get the house painted and at this rate it'll take all year.'

'But you've got on quickly enough by yourself,' she said.

'And I'm buggered.'

'But you don't need someone here doing it all week.'

'Well, you can't bloody do anything,' he said.

Bob didn't get up the next morning till about twelve, when he came down bleary-eyed and unshaven, and slumped at the table and read the Sunday papers and asked for coffee. Helen slammed it down in front of him. He looked up, sleepily.

'What's that for?'

'Oh God,' she said, 'you did ask for it.'

'Ask for what?'

'Coffee. Or didn't you?'

'I meant what did you slam it down for like that,' he explained, with vague annoyance; 'for?' he added, not sure whether he'd made the point.

'If you have to drink that much I don't see why you have to waste everyone else's time here while you sleep it off.'

'Who's everyone else's time?'

'How can I clean up if you want breakfast at this time of day?'

'I don't see that it makes any difference.'

'And how are we ever going to get the house painted at this rate? If you didn't go out and get drunk you wouldn't need to do stupid things like asking Colin to stay here.'

'Well I did ask him to stay here, so I can get drunk.'

And he did.

He had to go down for a drink that evening to settle the arrangements, and Colin agreed definitely to move in.

He moved in late Monday afternoon. He hitched from town, carrying his clothes in a canvas haversack.

'I've left my paintings at the pub,' he explained to Helen, 'and I said Bob and me would collect them this evening, I couldn't carry them on my own.' His boots sounded through the bare hall. 'Could be a nice little place,' he said, walking past Helen who still stood holding the door open. He unhitched the haversack and left it in the hallway, against the wall. 'I'll just dump this here, it'll be all right, no one'll pinch it,' he said, and walked on into the kitchen.

'I'd love a cup of tea,' he called out. Helen stopped by his haversack, but her hands couldn't touch the greasy stained canvas to move it out of sight.

'My mouth's sort of dried and furry after drinking at lunch.'

As she filled the kettle in the kitchen, he walked around the living room, his boots bumping against the chairs, which she had found in an antique shop and stripped and exposed as beautiful, bare wood. She was proud of the chairs, and of the old, long sofa she had found. He flopped down on it, and then got up to wander around again, scratching the black lead off the old cast-iron kerb around the hearth, that so suited the house, and that eventually would be a feature of the room.

'Why don't you take your boots off?' she said, restraining herself, keeping her voice controlled and neutral.

'Think you can stand the stink?' he asked, grinning.

'I hope so,' she said, preferring, then, anything to the thump and scratch. But she couldn't when he did take them off, and there was nothing, then, she could do about it, except perhaps take him for a bath and fumigate him. So she made tea, and sat saying nothing as he heaped in four spoons of sugar.

'I need the calories,' he grinned at her, owlishly behind his hideous spectacles. And he swung round on the sofa and put his feet up on it and with one long arm found a newspaper, and settled down to read.

When Bob got home they looked round the house. Helen had not offered to show Colin around, and anyway he had spent the afternoon dozing. They looked at the rooms, all unpainted and grubby. Bob started to shuffle and run his hands through his hair.

'I don't know where you're going to sleep,' he said, apologetic and vaguely helpless. 'Everything's such a shambles...'

'Oh,' Colin said, 'oh, I'm not worried about that. I've got a sleeping bag but it's down at the pub with my paintings. I thought we could pick them up tonight.'

'Bob's tired and needs some sleep; there's no point in going down there tonight,' Helen said.

And Colin generously agreed, disregarding Bob's incipient murmurings. 'Doesn't matter at all,' he said. 'I'll sleep on the sofa, it's comfortable and warm in there. If you've got a couple of blankets I'll be all right.

'Are you sure?' Bob asked. And when they left him Bob still worried.

'He's lucky to be able to sleep anywhere,' Helen said, 'and the sooner he gets his sleeping bag the better; he can put it in one of the rooms out of everyone's way. He can go and get it tomorrow.' And she tripped on the haversack in the hall at that, and screamed, and then cried. Colin opened the door.

'Are you all right?'

'She's okay,' Bob said, 'she just tripped.'

'I thought she might have miscarried or something.'

'I tripped on your haversack,' she said, and with all the venom she could she asked, innocuously, 'Don't you need it?' She had learnt at her school to put venom into innocuous phrases.

'No, you can dump it anywhere. There's nothing in it. I'll sleep in my underpants.'

And he said goodnight to them and shut the door.

Her eyes were dark, the brows and lashes strongly black, and the skin beneath her eyes slightly tinged with that darkness. So that if it did grow darker, Bob would not have noticed, and had he noticed, and noticed thought, he would have thought that perhaps pregnancy was making her tired. But he didn't notice, because if there was any darkening, it wasn't conspicuous, although she would sit in front of the mirror watching the lines deepen and the dark bruised shade spread outwards. There was no reason for him to look for any such a sign. Freed from the confinements of the flat he was happier, able now to go out in the evenings with Colin to the village pub, where they could chat and talk and drink and enjoy themselves.

'You're not driving Colin into town?' she had said.

'Why not?'

'Because you'll go buying him drinks and all his ghastly friends. Why do you need to go into town all the time?'

'I suppose we don't, really,' Bob said.

And indeed as the village pub was so pleasant, there was no need. So except for the evening when they went in to collect Colin's paintings – and he owed the barman there money anyway – they kept away.

'You know how much you owe me, Colin lad,' the barman said.

'Oh, Jack, come off it, I'll pay you back.'

'And pigs'll fly.'

'No, man, I'll let you have it. When I've finished these paintings…'

'Maybe I'll keep the paintings as security, like.'

'Oh, Jack, how can I ever make any money if you treat me like you're treating me, hey?'

Jack wouldn't speak when he was annoyed. He was enjoying this, making Colin wriggle.

'Where're you living now, anyway? How do I know you won't just pack your bags and do a runner?'

'I've nothing to pack.'

'Aye, and I'll make sure of that.'

'Tell you what, Jack, I'll let you keep the sleeping bag till I pay you. You wouldn't want to bug me by taking my paintings would you?'

'I don't know what I'd want to do, but I do know I don't bloody trust you an inch.'

So he kept the sleeping bag and Bob treated them to a drink on the strength of the agreement.

And after that they drank at the village pub, sitting in the public bar so that Colin could entertain the regulars with stories of his life. How in his London period, again when he had no money, he had shared a bed with an Irish tramp. And one night he picked up a girl, in a pub or coffee bar in Chelsea.

'Honest, man, she never washed. Paddy was bad enough, but she just never did. Real beat she was. So I picked her up and she said she wanted to come back with me so I thought, dig this, I thought, and then I thought, there's Paddy, but then I thought a bit more and decided it didn't make any difference really. It didn't either. He just lay there with his eyes shut pretending to be asleep. Anyway, I thought I'd better sleep in the middle – you know, man, like not that I didn't trust Paddy, I mean, I wouldn't've minded anyway, but he might have been shy. He was, too, real crazy.'

He cleaned his glasses on his shirt, holding his hearers in suspense, his long legs stretched under the table. He scratched his crotch.

'Never again, man. Like never. The bed sagged in the middle. And every time either of them moved – her or Paddy – they rolled into the middle. I was bloody sandwiched. Paddy wedged in on me on one side and her on the other. Never had a night like it. Honest, I nearly died of asphyxiation...'

And in the daytime he'd lie on the sofa until noon, reaching out a pallid arm for a newspaper or a cup of tea or coffee. Helen usually made coffee about eleven and she could think of no way to refuse to give him a cup. And so he would take one, his long white thin arm stretching out from beneath the blanket, the hairs of his armpit curling out just at the blanket's edge. And he would lie there, sipping his coffee, and examining his toes that he would stick out at the end of the sofa, white, unsunned toes with black-rimmed uncleaned toenails, like the broken teeth of a werewolf with strips of human flesh caught between them, rotting.

For three days he did a little work. He swept out one of the bedrooms and covered the walls with sugar soap; only at Helen's insistence that he couldn't slap paint straight onto that grime. And having covered the walls, mopping over them with a rag that he seemed to make unnecessarily dirty, he slumped to the floor, and then slumped through the house to the sofa, and sat there, drinking tea, and listening to the radio. Bob helped him wash the walls down in the evening, which took them about half an hour, and on the strength of that they went down to the pub.

He lay there, lolling, next morning. Helen dusted as he lay there, his eyes watching her move round, watching, not even saying anything, watching because she happened to be moving, as he watched his wriggling toes. She refused to ask him to get up.

'Do you want lunch in bed?' she asked, as she prepared to fry bacon and eggs.

'I'll get up,' he said, and arose from his blankets, his long white legs covered with grey hairs gripping them like dark seaweed, his underpants, aertex and frilly, hanging loosely from his hips and gaping open at the fly. She turned resolutely away and cracked eggs, and after a silent debate of conscience, left a splintered piece of eggshell in the pan.

For the next two afternoons Colin began to paint a room, beginning efficiently and surprisingly with the ceiling, which took some time, and working then on the walls. And when he had two walls finished, he made himself a pot of tea and carried it into the room and sat there, resting, in the lotus position.

She hated him for the unmade sofa, but couldn't bear the ruffled reminder of his pallid presence so she folded the blankets and sheets and put them in a cupboard herself, holding her breath. Each night he would get them out and assemble his bed, leaving the cupboard door swinging open, gaping.

But she couldn't refuse him his rest and admiring survey of his two walls and a ceiling. And after he had sat there with cigarettes and tea, he went to look for his paintings, canvas and board, and then, moving the paint cans out onto the landing, began to stand his paintings against the white walls. She knew this for certain when he came out to ask her where Bob kept a hammer and nails.

He squatted there, surveying his unfinished works, and chose finally the portrait of the girl he had been sleeping with who had given him the boot before he had finished painting her, and hung it centrally on the new white wall, hammering firmly in a couple of nails. On the other wall he hung two cubist attempts. The rest he left stacked against the skirting board, considering which to hang, and where, squatting amidst a circle of ash and butt ends and circular stains of the tea cup.

The next afternoon he set up an easel and put a painting on it, and carried a chair up from the kitchen and sat on it and smoked.

And he stayed. Helen would complain about his drinking with Bob every night, and Bob would simply reply, 'There's nothing to stop you joining us.'

'But I can't stand him,' she said, suddenly, desperately.

'Well I can,' Bob said, ruffling his hair and turning away as if he couldn't understand her, as if there wasn't any implication that she would have to learn to.

And they drank and became regulars with the locals, and perhaps once a week, at the weekend perhaps, they would drive into town for a drink.

She refused to do his washing. She refused to handle his filthy underpants, smelly, sweaty. She couldn't think of touching things he had worn next to his skin, the underpants he slept in and sat in and walked in. His hair was never cut, was thick and greasy. His nails were chipped, uneven, dirty. The combat jacket he had bought at an army surplus store was a symbol of dirt and fecklessness.

And he didn't paint. If he had painted she could have borne it, have tried to bear it; but he just sat in front of the picture of the awful girl he had had an affair with, just sat.

'Like man,' he offered her, an explanation she hadn't asked for but he wanted to give her, 'like man, like you're constipated, and you go to the john every day, two or three times a day, and nothing happens. And like you don't want to push it too hard in case, in case something happens, like you find a spot of blood in the pan. So you just keep on trying, gently like. Well, painting's like that.'

She picked up a pile of clothes and carried them out into the hall. He followed her, up the stairs, to the bedroom, still talking.

'Only with painting, like, you can't take liquid paraffin. Jeez, if only you could, like crazy, man. Whoosh.'

She put the clothes down and came out again, brushing past him as he stood right in the doorway, holding her body firm and rigid so that she mightn't touch him, drawing herself into her, even retracting the down on her arms. And with her breasts to the door-jamb, she brushed past him, feeling his warm, bad breath on the nape of her neck, which she washed in the bathroom – a new bathroom had been fitted before they moved in – while he carried on talking through the closed door.

'Course, sometimes painting's like diarrhoea. It all shoots out, all shapeless and formless; you've got all these ideas, all chewed up, and they come so quickly you haven't got time to sort of take them in your hands and mould them into shape. That painting of Sue, I had diarrhoea then.'

Back in the kitchen he ran the tap and filled the kettle to make tea, and when he'd done that, the noise ceased, he added, 'Literally, too. I'd get a couple of strokes on, and then, wham bam, I'd be fart-arsing down to the john.

'It's funny,' he said, 'I get a lot of my best ideas, just sitting there or peeing. I often get ideas when I'm on the beer and peeing out the back of the pub. Funny why they should come to you like that, isn't it? Must be something to do with peeing and fucking – you know, using it to create too.'

As he had hung up his paintings on the wall, he did not want to do any more to that room. It would mean moving everything he had hung up, and as there were lots of other rooms he could start on, it seemed pointless disturbing everything he had set out there. So he left it all, and began slowly to sweep out and sugar soap another room. It took him three afternoons. He got hay fever from the dust and had to go for a walk from which the rain drove him back, soaking, dripping water through the house, discarding wet clothing, and finally lying in scum and steam for half an hour in the bath, which he left covered with a soft grey fur crusted onto the enamel.

After that he took a walk most afternoons. He found it inspiring country, round the village and amongst the meadows. He didn't take a sketch book as he wasn't interested in painting landscapes, just in colour compositions, and he could take in the impressions of colour around the fields the more naturally without making sketches. And the mud would collect amongst the hob-nails of his boots and dry and fall off on the floor of the house in small curled segments.

'Look,' she said to him, pointing one afternoon.

He bent, peering through his glasses, and looked and picked up, curiously, the brown curled thing.

'What is it?' he asked, and sniffed it. 'Looks like rat turds to me.'
'Mud,' she said.
'Oh, mud,' and he tossed it into the sink, where the moisture eventually dispersed it into a sandy sediment.

The painting went slowly. And when Helen complained to Bob, he accused her of being bitchy and asked her how was it hurting her anyway. It wasn't that she was excluded. She could go drinking with them, there was nothing to stop that.

'I'm just *sick* of being left alone.'

'Well if you won't come out for a drink, what else do you expect? Anyway, you're not alone all day. Colin's here.'

'He's not even painting,' she said, 'he doesn't get out his paints or anything, he just sits and looks at that foul girl hanging there. He never makes any show of finishing it. I wouldn't mind his not painting the house if he was doing any of his own.'

'He's thinking, he can't paint all the time. He explained it to me, it's like…'

'I know, I know, I don't care, he's told me. You just don't realise, he lies in bed all day and does nothing. You're not here.'

'Well, he's not hurting you lying there. And you can't do anything, anyway, so he's not in the way of anything being done.' And his words prodded into her rounding belly, kicking her, so that she wanted to cry.

'The only time he does anything is when he goes to the Labour Exchange and gets his unemployment pay. It's dishonest.'

But it kept him in a reasonable amount of beer, and he studied the faces in the queues at the Labour Exchange.

'You mustn't limit the experiences life offers you,' he explained to Helen. 'You've just got to dig things.'

But the painting went slowly, even Bob admitted that. He stood in the hall and looked up the stairs to where there were rooms and rooms, floor upon floor. And only so slowly were they painting the corners of them, cleaning small patches of grime from the walls, preparing slight areas and sweeping floors that accumulated further dust. With all that weight of emptiness above and around he felt menaced, helpless. In the attic were old trunks full of junk, who knew what mouldering books and mildewed paintings, ornaments that held no attractiveness, candlesticks tarnished and blackened, chipped porcelain and children's toys. Beneath the windows plaster had crumbled from the damp; in the corners of rooms were cracks from subsidence. And there were outbuildings – laundries or stables or junk sheds. They could turn one into a barbecue, one into, perhaps, somewhere to sit, one into somewhere to put the baby's pram, out of the wind or the rain or the sun.

He went into the half-painted room where Colin's paintings hung. The girl looked at him, just looked at him. He wondered if that were a sign of Colin's skill, of his art, that she just looked, that she seemed neither firmly worse than she was, nor better, not idealised or etherealised.

He tried to think of what she was anyway, and came to no clearer discovery than that he had had in looking at the painting. But she was good company to drink with; they had drunk, he and Colin and her and all the others, through the pubs of the town, rolling arm in arm or clutching to shoulders and hands for support, through the half-timbered streets, driving past the river, singing from the tight-crammed back seat.

He looked at Colin's other efforts, stood back from them, considered them, the evening light coming palely through the sash-cord windows, and looked at the girl again, but her portrait meant nothing to him, told him nothing, brought simply a nostalgia for the rowdy nights.

'Jesus,' he said to Colin, who was lying on the couch in the living room, 'let's go into town tonight. I'm bored with the locals.'

'Sure thing,' Colin agreed.

They went round the cider pubs and got hideously, cruelly drunk. But not before they had arranged a painting party for the weekend, a blitz on the house to cover it with white paint, and lots of beer laid on.

Bill was a sort of Sunday painter when he wasn't too hung over from a Saturday night escaping his wife and kids and crawling around the pubs with Colin and Dave, who drove a delivery truck. Bob had joined their drinking group, which was generous and welcoming. Ray worked in an office in town and Pete when he did work was a truck driver. And there was John who had been educated at an expensive local private school and couldn't stand his family. They all arrived, in jeans and overalls and old trousers, in the morning, and they sugar-soaped and sandpapered and swept and painted, walls and ceilings and window frames and doors. They didn't open the first beer till some time after eleven, and then they'd have a drink when they were thirsty from the dust, and they opened a lot more bottles to go with the lunch that Helen served them after midday. She had bought a leg of ham and gave them salad, which they ate squatting on the floor, their hands and faces speckled with paint. She wouldn't eat anything herself. And when, after a few beers, they started again, she went round distastefully picking up scraps from the floor, stacking up plates with knives and forks left on them askew, gathering up bottles and bottle tops, and then washed up, swilling away gouts of tomato ketchup and salad cream, heaps of salt and fragments of hard-boiled egg.

As their enthusiasm waned and they drank more, they would tell jokes and roar with noisy laughter in the high-ceilinged rooms. They would sing, pop songs or travesties of operatic sounds, and guffaw or encore. The floors shook with the movement of their feet, with the scratching and dragging of tables and trestles. Doors left open to shout from room to room through would suddenly slam shut in a draught. And amongst it all Bob's laugh and voice were with the loudest.

The servants' staircase provoked merriment and bawdry, or communistic inveighing from Colin who was getting drunk. The memories of the august people who had first ever lived there were profaned with insult. The copulations performed in each bedroom were computed. Parties were canvassed and approved, wild orgies to involve Colin's former girl. 'We'll all go through her,' someone suggested, and the bare rooms sounded the approval. They would lay her on the splintered planks. Colin explained what had happened to the painting of her nude. Bill offered to paint both of them nude. 'I'll paint all three of you,' Bob shouted, and they all laughed.

'What are you going to do with Colin when you start having your smart cocktail parties?' Bill asked.

And they toyed happily with the idea of sending him up the servants' stairs, of dressing him as a butler, of pretending he was the gardener.

'Lucky old Lady Chatterley,' someone said, and they guffawed again, Bob and Colin especially.

And she sat there, trapped in her house, the home she was creating soiled by the white paint they flung with their dirty hands.

She sat there amongst her own whiteness, the cleanliness and isolation of the kitchen, looking at the furniture she had acquired and treasured, thinking of the home she had wanted and the child she had conceived, when Colin, who was in the next room, fell through the wall. Bill let out a mighty cheer and whoop, after the crash and crumble of the bricks and plaster, and called everyone else; they all came running, thundering down the stairs and hall, to gaze at the shattered wall, and to look through it at Colin lying in the rubble, swearing, cursing, and Helen, open-mouthed, screaming.

'He must be all right,' Bill said, 'just listen to him. Here, Colin lad, have a beer and sit up.' And he passed him a beer through the broken wall.

'Shitting fucking house,' Colin said.

'Are you all right?' Bob asked, blinking, rubbing the hair and haziness from his eyes with a paint-smeared hand, coming through the kitchen door.

'Never mind him, what about me?' Helen said.

'What's the matter with you?'

'I might have miscarried,' she said, and as he looked at her, slumped in a chair, her eyes dark and heavy, he felt a sudden concern.

'Come to bed and lie down then,' he said, while everyone else was turned to Colin.

'How can I with all this to clear up?'

'Well if you can clear all this up you can't have miscarried,' and he turned away adding, hurtfully, 'can you?' – not even you – and bent to Colin.

'Bloody winded,' Colin said. His side and back were white; it had been a just-painted wall that he had tripped and fallen through.

They climbed through the hole and sat on the floor, sipping beer and wondering what to do and Helen sat in a chair in the kitchen, looking at them through the hole. And after that, after sitting down together and drinking, everyone felt too exhausted to do any more that day and it was five o'clock anyway so they began to clean the paint from their hands to go out for the evening. Helen refused to cook. 'How can I with that mess everywhere?'

'I'll clean it up tomorrow and rebuild the wall at the same time,' Bob said as he left her to go off with the others for a Chinese meal. They drank till closing time and came back with bottles to carry on drinking, and in the morning Pete and Dave and John were sleeping on rugs and cushions and Colin was snoring on the sofa and in every room were dried, uncleaned paint brushes and paint-stepped footmarks in the hall and when Helen reached the bathroom, it was locked. She knocked on the door, her face set, her teeth clenched.

In a couple of minutes it was opened and Colin's girl, more ravaged than her portrait, stood in the doorway groaning. 'I've just been sick,' she said.

Bob was busily making coffee to relieve the hangovers when there was a hooting outside.

'Jesus,' he said, wincing, 'what the hell's that?'

'It's all right,' Helen said, 'I'll see to it,' and went out, shutting the front door behind her. The strangeness of that slowly registered, and Bob shambled to the front windows, to see a taxi going out of the gateway.

'Jesus,' he said, and looking at the wrecked kitchen wall and the unshaven faces amongst the rugs and cushions, he tugged at his hair for a moment before he poured the coffee.

Helen communicated with him later, announcing that she wouldn't be coming back from her mother's until Colin had left and the wall had been rebuilt and the place was fit to live in. This required little arrangement, as Colin moved back in with his girl the following night, and Bob drove them back, together with the paintings, into town, and got a jobbing builder from the village to reconstruct the wall, and the definition of making the place fit to live in was reasonably subjective and flexible, and anyway she wouldn't have wanted him to do things she had planned to do on her own. And Bob then went off the beer till the baby was born, which wasn't long anyway. And he couldn't go out much afterwards, because of the problem of getting baby sitters.

The Decline in Importance
of the Family

As I climbed the station steps to the platform, automatically I looked at the girls coming down, wearing their straw boaters and swinging their bulky satchels on their shoulders; automatically – because the age differential was now somewhat important, in one's home town, automatically because it was the conditioned reflex of ten years' growing up looking at the same girls on the cycle ride into school. I'd been looking at them that morning as I cycled into the station and when I became aware of it, I was surprised at my unconscious reaction. I hadn't cycled down at that particular and reflex-promoting time for quite a while. It was a forgotten routine, and to be reminded of it in some way made up for cycling in the suit I'd pressed the night before.

There were numerous *Mirrors* and *Expresses* on the station bookstall, but for the interview I thought a knowledge of current affairs might be required. It was a bit desperately late in the day to gain any, except the most current and undocumented by any previous reading of the events, but it was a gesture towards the seriousness of the occasion. As the train was only just coming into sight down the line, I scampered over the footbridge to the larger stall on the other platform. *The Guardian* perhaps was not the best choice, but current affairs or no, I wanted something to fill in the three hours; and it would look more with-it on the journey, compensate minimally for the baggy bottoms of the interview suit. With the express arrived and the engine hissing below, I stood again on the footbridge and looked at the film set of rails and junctions and lines stretching out distantly; it was still an emotionally potent shot, not that I was feeling any emotion particularly, but had I been, this would have suited it; except that the anonymity and uniformity of the stations meant that any symbol of departing from the known and loved native land, the well-worn streets and oft-trod river banks, would lose its effectiveness, because all the home-town connotations were missing on the barren platforms and girdered roofs. The station was fine for desolation and tears, but it could not suggest what actually was lost, the missing chunk that caused the deprivation. But rather than miss the train and stay in the home town, I moved on.

The hope of a county bird alone in a carriage with her *Tatler* was always present; wanted because, I think, unknown and impossible, not for anything intrinsic, wanted because of the difference from the ubiquitous and scrappy city sparrows. Either that, some two-legged erotic fantasy, or an empty carriage to read and doze in. Saying goodbye were a cluster of what seemed to be what I meant; two of about my own age and sex, and a girl with an overnight case. I walked towards them, to glimpse and pass by and perhaps reflect on the fantastic.

But it wasn't quite like that, because as I approached she waved and her brother David waved and Simon waved and I waved back.

If from that lone sentinel's position on the footbridge I had been watching us, waving, I would have gripped my *Guardian* more tightly for consolation and reassurance. We would have stood there for the right things.

'Hello,' she said.

'How are you, Mike?' said her brother.

'Hello, then,' said Simon.

And then there was a silence after my interrupting their not saying anything in particular, whose thread it was difficult to pick up.

'Are you catching the train?' she said.

'Yes.'

'No, I'm just seeing her off,' said her brother, blinking his eyes as a comment on having got up so early.

I wondered whether to move on or stay. I didn't want to intrude on something, on someone's privacy, or on something between Simon and her, though I was pretty sure there wasn't anything. Yet to go away out of this ridiculous deference – the sort of nervousness I had always felt of her when we were at school – would be to have a three-hour train journey on my own. I argued it out silently – after all, I did want to talk to them both, whom I'd not met for perhaps two years; and finally I raised the possibility that if I went off on my own, they would wonder at my unsociability, rather than wondering at my nervousness. And unsociability was something I felt misrepresented me. Lately arguments with myself were becoming more easily won.

'Sorry,' I said, 'I wasn't listening.' And then, 'No, I'm going up to London too. I've got a damn interview.'

'Oh, so's Simon,' she said, at the same time as he said, 'So've I.'

We listened to the hissing steam again. Doors were slammed on carriages down the train. A few heavy mailbags were dropped against a wall. There was noise of pigeons from a crate marked 'With Care'.

'Well, I'm going back to bed,' said her brother.

'Thanks awfully for bringing me,' she said, 'sorry to drag you up at such an unearthly hour. And thank the parents, won't you; they've been awfully good, sorry I couldn't say goodbye to them – do tell them, won't you; they'll understand. Why don't you come up with Jan some time and see the flat. We could put you up or something. Why don't…?'

Simon and I looked at each other. 'Well,' we asked each other, 'how are things?' 'Not so bad,' we said.

'And let me know how your exams go. I'll let you know when I'm coming home. I'll phone through, or something. Bye for now. Give my love to Jan. Bye.'

We said goodbye to her brother and let her get on the train first. Simon took her weekend case.

It was one of those carriages that wasn't in compartments, but was completely open, more like a bus or a tube. We found seats at the end. She and Simon sat on one side of the table between the double seats, I sat opposite them. Slowly the train moved out, and from the confines of the station buildings the view expanded to the still small canal, the scrap yard with the broken shells of cars stacked at the water's edge, the gasworks with its huge bunkers of coal and with the great ferroconcrete structure whose function could not even be surmised, the odd Georgian house, trapped by the railway and canal, blackened, and turned into flats. The cathedral stood beautifully, framed by the chimneys and coal chutes. It looked odd, because here still the cathedral represented the town and the chimneys were later excrescences on the old ecclesiastical lands and fertile soil.

'He is a dear,' she said. 'The parents were still in bed, but he got up and cooked me breakfast and drove me down.'

'How long have you been home for?' I asked.

'Twenty-four hours.'

The time unit rather gave her away, showed she knew it was odd and showed she designedly made it odd, rather than mundanely 'Just a day'; however mundane to her that brief trip to the parents might be – mundane in its brevity – she drew attention to the back of the poster with the props bolted on the frame, holding up the hoardings to passing travellers, by saying, so clearly consciously, twenty-four hours. Though she made her point, still.

'You're not going back today?' she asked.

'No; no, I've got another week.'

'How long have you been home?'

'Three.'

I felt ashamed of it.

'I stayed up for two weeks, but…'

'Oh, I couldn't stand it at home. The parents are dears, but you know. There's so much to do in London.'

She emphasized the do. An active girl. An alive girl.

'I mean here' – she indicated the fowl pens at the bottoms of the gardens – 'there's just nothing.'

My position had to be made clear.

'I know – it's grim; but I've got plenty of work to do.'

'I can't work at home,' she said.

'I can't work anywhere,' Simon smiled at us, his almost buck-teeth grinning. 'Anyway, I can't afford to. It's too expensive to stay up in the vacs.'

She started talking about her overdraft. I didn't have an overdraft, and I think that even if I had, I wouldn't have talked about it. The way I had been brought up, you didn't have overdrafts; having a bank account was exceptional enough. You never used to have enough money to put in a bank, and you would never have dared to run into debt. I was getting more than a bit fed up with the way I had been brought up, but I was glad that I didn't have an overdraft. She hadn't been brought up quite the same way; that had been evident when we were both at school, different schools, at the same time.

'Still,' she said, and she laughed. It was an odd laugh, it was very near to a 'Huh-huh', the guffaw of the pint mug; it came from the depths like that. But it was controlled, modulated I suppose is the word. It had its upper reaches, its soprano, but you remembered it by the guffaw element that was no guffaw. Her voice, too, was soft, gentle and low, yet with this ungentle penumbra. She modelled her natural vocalics onto some sexy husky norm. But she might have modelled them onto the resonant harshness of the market stall; she didn't, never even if hysterical would she, reach that coarseness; but the penumbra hovered hauntingly behind, giving her the attraction of this ambivalence. It went, anyway, with her sun-browned skin, her brown eyes, and rather lovely dark hair. If she ever went to the bad that they might hear of back home, back in our mutual youthful environment, they would say that after all, she was only half English. Which was true.

'I'd like a lot of money,' she said. She'd pulled up the sleeves of her neat black jersey to the elbows. Propping her chin up on her clasped hands, the elbows resting on the table but cushioned by the double thickness of the turned-back cuff of her jersey, she looked as attractive as I'd always thought her – and that wasn't true of everybody. With the brown skin, the clear beautiful complexion, went dark un-English hair on her arms and slightly on her upper lip. I was surprised at this, she didn't seem the sort of girl to have hair noticeably on her arms, legs or lip; and if she did have it, she wasn't the sort of girl to let it remain there.

The wish for a lot of money, naive in someone else, with her seemed natural. You rather though expected her already to have a lot of money, not still to be wanting it. She'd always managed to keep the wealthy and unpleasant bastards interested in her at home.

I remembered that Simon had gone out with her, which was odd. He wasn't after all a bastard. It was unfortunate really that his name was what it was, especially as it couldn't be abbreviated. He was pleasant, quiet, nervous, but that never seemed to worry him. He'd taken her out, after all.

He started talking about the number of people who were thrown out every year from his course. I didn't like people to identify me or the people I was with as a student, as anything, and we were in an open carriage. I was conscious that the passengers around could hear us – if they bothered to listen, of course. Still, it was interesting to hear how many people were thrown out every year from his course. I didn't know how many people were thrown out from mine, or even if any were. It was hardly a pressing problem. The way I had been brought up you couldn't afford to waste two years and get thrown out before your finals, so you didn't get into that sort of position.

She found it easier working in London than at home, and anyway there were a lot more other things to do in London. She looked very much the sort of girl who knew lots of things to do in London, with that black jersey, with the sleeves casually pulled up to the elbow, and that slim black skirt. I couldn't see her legs because of the table but I remembered they were good and I remembered when I first caught sight of her she had been wearing dark net stockings. I'd thought black was rather going out; all the smart girls I knew by sight seemed to have abandoned it; maybe it was coming back in again. She didn't give the impression of a girl who would allow herself to be wearing anything at all out. For us provincials, in fact, she was very much in; she knew she was one up on us by living in London, and though I would have hated that, I accepted her scoring; and she knew she was another one up on us by coming home to the parents for only twenty-four hours. I rather envied her that one. I was getting tired of many of the many ways I had been brought up. But then, London was London, and our older universities in vacation time were not very different from our home towns. She rather wanted to make it clear to us she was quite in; quite what she was in it was not possible to decide at present; but she wanted not to make her travel tales too obviously introduced, and neither of us seemed to have a lead in for her to begin. Three years was a long time for us all to have been separated from a none-too-close togetherness. I would have liked to have heard, both from a vicarious interest in living (and, exams over, I was intending to live in her sense, even if not her way), and from a gossipy curiosity in local girl making something; onto the parochial gossip in which I had been brought up, I had grafted a ready absorption of sleaziness and sexual mores, built up from the gossip columns and contemporary fiction, and the curious environment of our older universities. Simon, too, was eager to tell of his life and the problem here was to hold him off. He was training to be a civil engineer. I felt that in her world of art schools and metropolitan vice, there might be more of interest than in the clean new concrete dams or the un-metaphorical sadly concrete sewers. There wasn't much about myself I wanted to offer – people aren't very interested in permitted disclosures and in that company I preferred to yawn than be yawned at. It might have shown the fillings in her teeth. So we sat, in something of an impasse, with words sliding vaguely between us, as the train lurched rhythmically and people talked through the un-partitioned carriage.

The arrival of a restaurant car waiter offering coffee made the transition; having agreed to coffee – for me, on a train, the way I had been brought up, something of a let's be wicked residuum still remained – we agreed to a new chattiness. To hell with current affairs. Simon talked about an interview he had been up to London for two weeks earlier. She told us how her flat had been burgled. The wicked city. An imagined debauch of scattered gin bottles and underwear, drawers flung open and their contents strewn around, a window loose with the curtain flapping after the soft-soled housebreaker. Simon had lost a transistor radio; someone had walked into his hall of residence and lifted wallets and easily portable items, and walked away again no doubt with a full suitcase.

We talked of old friends we had known. One had called in on her flat – she had given him her address – one night just as she was going out; it was rather late as, from his state, the pubs seemed to have shut; but she was just going out; it was rather difficult, she said. Fortunately he, and the two or three he was with, had somewhere else to move on to.

But calling on anyone that time of night, she repeated, especially when you're just going out, makes things embarrassing. 'I mean,' she went on, to make her point clear, 'I couldn't say make yourselves at home till I come back because I wasn't, well, you know; but, anyway, still, they'd somewhere else to go to.'

The confusion of monosyllables and her laugh was attractive. She gazed out of a window to the high green bank of a cutting, gazing blankly as if recalling against that green screen the images of some past event and evening. The coffee arrived and was poured in the swaying carriage with the minimum of spilling. To hold the cup was something for hands to do. She held hers with both hands, leaning her elbows on the table, and looking across the top of the cup with those dark, remembering eyes. She hadn't noticeably plucked her eyebrows. We started talking about jobs. Simon knew a lot of people who were starting off as engineers at nine hundred a year. She knew lots of people who were starting off at eleven hundred. She was starting at a thousand, next year. It had all been arranged. 'I shall just do it for a year,' she said, 'and then go to Italy or somewhere; Florence, I think. Oh, it's wonderful. But I could do with some money for a year, I'm so tired of being broke.'

It had been arranged. She was lecturing at some London art school. The principal seemed to have taken a fancy to her, as they'd say at home. That was the impression she gave. 'I went to see him,' she said, 'and had a sort of casual interview; and then he asked me out to dinner; and then he asked me out again. And the third or fourth time I said, you know if you don't take me this is going to be awfully expensive.'

'So he took you,' Simon said.

'Yes,' she said, 'eventually.'

He could hardly be blamed. Maybe, on this thousand a year, she could, if black really was not with it, buy whatever colour was. Though of course black suited her, dark and slim.

Amidst this life of burglars and going out late, of wining and dining and large start-up salaries, Simon seemed hard to place. That once he had gone out with her for two weeks or so, had danced at the barbecue amidst the bushes of the vicarage garden, and partnered her in the gymnasium at her school's summer dance, that once there had been some degree of something between them, could never have been inferred from seeing them there. She'd been, for me at any rate, the sort of girl who was too sophisticated for her years, too condescending, too unnerving. Her act had always convinced me, even when I'd known so well it was an act. It's no good going onto the stage and shouting 'It's all lies,' because people will hiss and get you flung out; the only thing to do is to put make-up on as well, and then people will think it's part of the show; and then you've got your own act and are in a position to confront the others. But I never came up with that sort of public act. Nor really did Simon. He smiled and was nervous, but was driven by this simple liking for attractive girls. For her, that was all past. My adolescent blushes and nervousness when anywhere in her company, like sorting letters at Christmas at the post office, and his Babychams bought before the school dance, all were equally in the past and forgotten by her, belonging to the cemetery to which she'd paid a twenty-four hour visit to breathe fragrant flowers over her parents' tomb. And what for me had been a long embarrassment, and for Simon something of a triumph – as far as we ever knew – both equally were forgotten. She was a different girl in a different town; we were friends to talk to on a tedious journey, but as she looked back through the carriage window, the tracks we had followed and were travelling along had no interest for her in where they had been, at what level crossings they had waited, at what junctions they had come in, in where they were leading, or at what deserted now long since closed down halt, with the forget-me-nots spreading over the platform, they had lain close to hers; that age of steam had passed. And having realised all this, and happy, happy to be accepted as the present, I drank down my coffee and wondered how to put Simon at his ease, without at the same time encouraging him to autobiography. The restaurant-car waiter passed down the carriage again for payment; after the fumble for money in trouser pockets inconvenient when sitting down, Simon paid for himself and for her, and I paid for my own.

I started to catch up on current affairs and Simon pulled out a notebook on sewers. They began talking about them, till she began to look at one of her art history set texts. There weren't many current affairs of interest, so I watched her with the book open in front of her, looking out of the window as we passed telegraph posts and gangers' huts, cryptic notices of mileages and gradients, sheep nibbling grass, and occasionally winding rivers we would cross and cross again. It looked very restful and it was not wholly clear to me how she could enjoy living all the time in London. Perhaps she didn't need injections of chlorophyll for the dried-up mouth after nights of gin and whisky; or maybe she got it with her toothpaste. I began to read about rehousing army regulars. When I'd finished that she was still looking at the telegraph posts. We started to talk again because in that open carriage it was difficult to concentrate on anything else with people on other seats talking all the time. We talked of university libraries and of the glories of Florence, of her flat which cost four pounds a week and my room which was thirty bob, of little places she knew where you could eat wonderfully or where lovely things could be got cheaply. We passed sheep and trees and cattle and occasionally people would get in at the few stations our express stopped at. Passing a sewage plant, Simon explained how it worked, which was interesting as I didn't know and wondered what the circular concrete structures were. We remembered people we had been at school with who had achieved fame or got married or done well, and we came nearer London, through the miles of factories for paint brushes and eau de cologne, through the masses of dormitory suburbs and cemeteries, where the only green stuff was in the occasional park with swings and paddling pools.

'What time's your interview?' she asked.

They were both at two.

'Why,' she asked, 'why don't you come round to the flat then? I'll cook something, you don't mind a sort of scrap meal? There should be something there somewhere. I've got to go out this afternoon but not till about three. Would you like to, or are you doing something?'

Simon looked at me and I looked back as if we needed each other's permission. Imperceptibly we nodded, conspiratorial as aliens in another town.

'Sure,' he said. 'Love to,' I said. And she smiled at us, 'Good.'

As we came into Paddington I picked up her suitcase and followed her into the corridor. It was, of course, damn heavy, and standing there in the decelerating train, wedged in the corridor, its weight began to ache down on my fingers. She told me she'd got books in it; she was gradually collecting the few remaining possessions of hers that she had left at the parents', and transporting them up to the flat.

'It's not too much, is it?' she asked.

The expanse of Paddington, the masses of people pouring out of the train, the masses of people pouring out of different trains on different platforms, was striking as ever. Why, I wondered, were they all arriving? We walked along the platform, beneath the high girders, and Simon stopped at a timetable. He dictated the times of the trains back home and I wrote them down on my Post Office Bank book. 'Shall we get a taxi?' she said. 'There's enough of us and it'll be easier with the case.' We thought about it and she clearly preferred a taxi to dragging down into the underground or climbing to the top of a bus. So we got a taxi and were out of the station amidst the populous streets, the high houses and pressing shops, the milling people and mass of road signs, people and taxis, particularly taxis, moving in swarms along the roads. She sat in the middle and Simon and I looked out of the windows. I was surprised he looked out with such evident interest. She gave instructions on where we had to go. It was little things, like the traffic streams, two or three abreast where at home they would go in one straggly line; or wider roads and higher buildings; or people stretching indefinitely. The main streets just went on and on, into greater or lesser main streets; there were no county libraries or shire halls to leave unlocked bicycles at instead of paying a parking fee at the station.

'I thought,' I said, because I'd just remembered it, or wasn't sure whether I had remembered it or whether I had confused some other memory, 'you'd got engaged or something.'

'Me?' she said, and looked with that bright-eyed wide-mouthed smile, and gave that laugh. She leant her elbows on her knees which obtruded from the black hem of her skirt, and leant her chin on her clasped hands, looking ahead over the driver's shoulder, going more serious and reflective.

'No,' she said, 'I nearly was, though. I – oh,' and she stopped, filling in the interim with some movement or gesture before starting again. 'It was – well, I might have done, but I didn't; that's why I've got so much work to do now, it messed me up for quite a time.' She'd been saying on the train how much work she had to do before her finals and how rather worried she was.

It was difficult to decide whether she wanted to be asked further about her mystery, her sad past, whether, like her life of doing things in London we had come across on the train, she had given a hint so that we would make the further inquiries without her having to offer them unsolicited, that she might not seem to be holding forth with the conceit of a big city girl too blatantly, whether, that is, she wanted to tell us but was aware of a certain decorum in these things and so wouldn't force those faded riotous blooms on us; or whether further inquiries would be intrusive and unwelcome, and further revelations made to further inquiries made only by her under the stress of remembered emotion and to be regretted afterwards. Simon was no help; he sat there, also wondering. And her hip stuck into mine and no doubt her other hip into his in the back seat of the taxi, so that it would be illegitimate to imagine a special intimate pressure.

She had an exchange of ideas with the taxi driver whose import I didn't bother to follow. Traffic was everywhere. A van had stalled in the middle of the road. Shops shrieked their offers together, deafening each other, so that they produced a bitty kaleidoscope of posters and bargain offers. And over the shop fronts were two or three storeys of dark windows, where mobsters planned raids and rammed the solid taxis, where old ladies died, where models entertained, where students with lovely legs shared digs. The mass of shops interspersed with banks and marble-fronted pubs stretched on and on. The taxi pulled up, quite arbitrarily, for everywhere was the same and repeated itself, and being nearest the kerb I clambered out, with the twenty-four hour case. We clustered by the pavement edge. 'Just time for a quick one,' the driver said to her, nodding to the green-glazed front of a pub we had stopped by. She smiled and Simon and I did a quick pool of money. I let him pay and calculate the tip. We never used taxis at home. I don't think Simon did, either, but he'd once had a job driving one for a few weeks.

On the train she had told us there was a club in the basement and a showroom for something on the ground floor. We walked along the pavement a little and then turned in, among the caravans. Why anyone should want a caravan showroom in the centre of London it was difficult to imagine. It was obviously a front for something dodgy. At the back was a cardboard or plywood stage set of palm trees and pirate treasure. The hole that coincided with the mouth of a cave was the entrance to the club. On the other side was a doorway. We went through it and on to damp, carpetless stairs. An empty unwashed milk bottle had been abandoned at the bottom. There were no lights and the stairs twisted around. And then there was a landing where a small pane of frosted glass, dusty inside and grimed with rain-washed smoke and soot outside, illuminated a short corridor. We went along it, standing on the light coloured centre strip which had once been covered by a carpet, and stood while she fumbled for a key.

And the door open, we were into her flat and the darkness. She crossed the room and switched on a light there. It was narrow, the room, and at the end where she stood was another door that led, presumably, to her flatmate's room. Some light came in through a small window next to the door where we had come in. I made a right-hand turn to look through it and faced a high, blank brick wall, about a yard away. The room was the width of that door and that window, with a few fragments of wall extra. And at right angles to the window was a half-open door that led into, clearly, the kitchen.

From the light of the table lamp she had switched on I could see the darker recesses of the room where she stood – the light from the window would hardly have illuminated anything. There was a single bed with one end of it against the flatmate's wall, and the side of it pushed up close to the kitchen wall. It served as a couch in the daytime. There was a full bookcase, a record player on the floor, a table against the wall opposite the bed, and scattered on the table and floor, books and sheets of paper, odd boxes and packets and ashtrays, a copy of *Queen*, and general, unspecific things. There were prints on the walls.

Simon had disappeared into the kitchen, looking round like a brother, but she still stood at the one end of the room, stroking a stockinged foot against a woolly white rug. The table lamp made her complexion bronze where the light caught it and shone ripples on her jersey. She was reading a letter which she must have picked up from somewhere. 'Oh God,' she said. She'd made the flat very pleasant. A lightless hovel, she had made it arty with the prints and things and on the bookshelves in front of the books, and on the table the lamp was on, ornaments and acquisitions, shells and carvings. The inevitable wax-dipped champagne bottles were on the mantelpiece of a blocked up fireplace. I suppose I should have expected them but I had imagined they were clearly out of fashion even for phoneys. Perhaps she just liked them, like wearing black. The bric-à-brac was not so much of the art student – those I'd met seemed not to have many possessions – but of the artistic girl. She'd said on the train she had shared a flat earlier with four or five girls who were rather debby; and this was the suggestion of this junk. It was difficult to distinguish between the arty, who after all was not very different from the jolly or the horsey, and the connoisseur. I think she rather wanted to be the latter, and the conscious frugality of her lack of personal ornament fitted that. In the same sort of way the flat was tidy, despite the boxes and papers and things. The disarray of gin bottles and underwear had been cleared up. As it was small perhaps it had to be kept tidy, though my thirty bob a week digs weren't; but then, I didn't invite people back for omelettes. Though even had I done, and even as I did, asking them back for other things, I felt that untidiness made the squalor somehow attractive, a touch of the bohemian. I don't think she was that really. Bohemian. Except on her mother's side, who had come over as a refugee.

'Oh dear,' she said, 'poor girl.'

And looking up, expecting to see me looking at her inquiringly and seeing me looking at her inquiringly, she said, 'It's Madeleine, she shares the flat,' and she nodded indicatively towards the other bedroom, 'she's just broken off her engagement.'

She looked at the letter again, skimming over the sheet as if expecting to find, well, to find something, perhaps.

'I knew it would happen,' she said, 'They've been engaged nearly three years – soon after she came here. Poor girl. I wonder when…'

She looked at it again.

'Sunday. I saw her Saturday. Oh well, it's probably for the best. I suppose.'

She folded the letter and put it back in the envelope. The envelope was unstamped and must have been left on the bed. She opened the handbag she had left on the big table and put the letter in and closed the bag and put it back on the table and took her foot out of her other shoe and went into the kitchen.

'Can you see any food, Simon?' she said. It was a nice voice and I was surprised that she didn't say 'Simon dear' as people with that sort of voice usually did.

'Well,' he said, 'I haven't really looked.'

Their voices came to me from the kitchen as I crouched down to look at the books. I noticed she had a life of Ruskin that I'd also got, picked up from a rummage sale, and often wondered whether to throw away as it looked useless; as she had it, and perhaps knew what was, or should be, good, I decided to keep my copy. She'd brought, as she'd said when I held the suitcase, nearly all the stuff from home up to the flat bit by bit; this was clear from the books which showed her old interests, her growing up in serge skirts and a boater, a growing up at the same time as Simon and I had been growing up. She must have been interested in the same sort of things when she was younger as I had been; funny I'd never known. Though of course she had been interested in other things too; and participant in them, which rather made the difference. A few of the books were in French which looked rather good, though they seemed to belong to that past when she had gone on holiday to stay with her penfriend. She looked through from the kitchen. 'Put a record on, Mike,' she said, 'have a look through them.' I began to look through the pile of glossy sleeves. 'We really,' she said back in the kitchen, 'need some milk.'

'I'll get it,' Simon said; the trouble about being chivalrous is that you have to go on errands for the lady, leaving her surrounded by the unchivalrous and lazy bastards who nobly try to keep her entertained and amused in your absence.

'Would you?' she said. 'Oh, thanks awfully, it's not far…' which rather took the glamour off the exploit. 'And do you think you could get a loaf? There's a shop…'

And while I heard the unimportant instructions I looked on through the records. Thanked, Simon went out and down the damp and gloomy stairs. She smiled at him and closed the door and came over to the records.

'They're not,' she said, 'all mine. Someone lent me them.'

She managed always to make her implication clear in what she said. It was clearly some man friend who had lent her them. It wasn't that that was important, but the way in which she was able to imply it. It was skilfully done, more skilfully done than some of her earlier implications on the train; though the thing implied, her necessity for implying that it was a man friend, seemed, as I felt with the others, clumsy. Why, after all, bother? She crouched down, and her knees in her net stockings were as I kept on noticing good and their disappearance beneath the black, slim skirt provocative. She leant across me to pick up some records and her knee rubbed against mine in its wretched interview suit. I'd already taken off my jacket to try and forget it was a suit; she didn't move away suddenly from the unexpected contact so, thinking, nor did I. So, knees touching, we talked about records or something. The consciousness of it was liable to set the nerve in my leg quivering as I was crouched uncomfortably, and if that happened I'd have to move. I didn't want to, though what could be gained I couldn't see; what was the point of it? Or had she, perhaps, not noticed. The possibilities raced around and I kept my knee still. I longed for the nineteenth century where, according to my reading, this sort of thing would have been impossible, or for the eighteenth where one would have known what it meant and what to do next.

'This is great,' she said, holding the record of the theme of *Jules et Jim*.

I rather expected she might like that; I'd liked that song, too. A capital city, a flat, a femme fatale and the glamour, these appealed. She went over to the record player and switched its various switches on. She opened the other bedroom door.

'That's Madeleine's room,' she said.

It was rather lighter, brighter, though not quite as big. There was a copy of *Woman* by the bed. I wondered how they managed, those two who had so nearly got married. Whether they had all night foursomes, in separate rooms; or whether it was all strictly last century and hometown underneath; and it was a speculation in which there was no information to help me. Her earlier flat with four or five others, that seemed clear enough. Impropriety was for her inconceivable in a shared bedroom; but she had moved on from it; and to have moved to a flat on her own would have been expensive and, possibly, despite all her friends, lonely. Madeleine for a while now would be lonely except for sharing the flat with her.

I turned round and going back through her room, stepping over the shed shoes, went into the kitchen where she was cracking eggs into a basin. It was like London, the cosmopolitan populousness; onions hung against a shelf, sticks of spaghetti poked out of a blue wrapping, Italian and unusual and stocked in our home town only at the rather esoteric quality grocers, tins of things, saucepans, unwashed plates, everything crowded, such dense heterogeneity that looked at from a distance it would seem a homogeneous matted texture, a plastered wall with the shapes of the apparatuses of modern living impressed and moulded in a modern khaki artwork.

'Don't look,' she said.

There were mops and brushes; there was a curtained-off bath; an oven; a chair or so; everything reaching right to the ceiling, shelves with debby and arty and un-English foods rubbing against potatoes and bags of British Sugar Corporation sugar. It was small and there wasn't really a lot, in bulk; but the mass and variety, the density, with *Jules et Jim* drifting through the wall, impressed me as something I'd not known before.

Simon arrived back with bread and milk.

'Fantastic,' he said, 'I've never seen people queuing for bread before, not for years. Hundreds of them, all sorts, outside the shop on the pavement.'

She smiled. 'Oh, yes.'

'Never seen it since the war,' he said. 'Fantastic.'

She offered no reason, perhaps there wasn't one. Perhaps they had just baked, perhaps it was good bread. Simon shook his head and gave an amazed, amused, and above all satisfied chuckle; odd things are satisfying, some of them.

And so I speculated, as she made omelettes and Simon helpfully cut bread and changed the records. And every so often, shuddering in my stomach, came the fact of the interview I was here for. It was fortunate, I thought, coming to after all of it the purpose of the dark suit, that I had had something to fill in the time between the train's arrival and the appointment, between the train's departure and the appointment. I would rely, I decided, on my wits rather than on current affairs. I wondered where Madeleine was, at home and broken-hearted, or consoling herself desperately in some other flat, or living it up with some more engaging man than her former fiancé.

For all its attractiveness of having been rescued from the rubbish heap and refurbished and made so nice, the flat was anonymous, lived in, yes, but none of the appurtenances of living that archaeologists always find in heaps around excavated villages, bones and needles and coal and broken urns; nothing of that was here, no trimmings of nails nor scraps of half-used paper, no out-of-date invitations waiting mournfully to be replaced by a current one, no piles of useless periodicals that somehow weren't thrown out because there was possibly something in them to keep.

There wasn't an uncomfortable tidiness and polish; but nor was there a sense of – to use inescapably the word – home. What, exactly, a sense of home would be, I found it difficult to imagine and probably a sense of home would have distressed me. The way I had been brought up we had a very strong sense of home. Still, as we ate rather delicious omelettes, which I remembered to congratulate her on, not too soon which would have looked unconvincing with having tried only half a mouthful, so I had to eat two or three mouthfuls, more quickly than normal, conscious of her rather expecting and waiting for approval but determined when I did express it not to bungle it, still, there was something missing; there was no key to the sort of life she was leading and home certainly always shows that. More, though, it seemed that she herself wasn't sure of what life she was leading, or wanted to lead, so tried a number of them. I didn't blame her, but it must have been something of a strain, especially when she seemed definitely to want some certainty, wasn't resigned to paddling in every pool and avoiding total immersion. I began to feel sorry for her.

We talked at ease over the coffee and it wasn't just as if three years had been caught up on but as if we had met for the first time on a train or in a dance only recently and were talking relaxedly. When someone knocked on the door we were all rather annoyed as it broke into the chatting on the comfortable chairs and white rug.

'Come in,' she said, not really bothering.

He came in, with glasses and a cool modern haircut and an Italian style suit, carrying a large bundle wrapped in paper. She stood up, bare-footed, put her hands to her eyes.

'It's...' and thinking, she smiled and eventually hazarded, 'Denis.'

'That's it,' he said, a cockney, 'I've brought the stuff.'

'The table's all right,' she said, 'don't bother about all that,' and she moved some of the clutter from the top of it. He put down his parcel, looked round and smiled at us.

'Hi,' he said. 'I'm not interrupting, am I?' he asked her.

'No, no, it's quite all right.'

And he unwrapped the paper.

'This is the stuff, anyway,' he said. 'I dunno whether it's quite what you wanted.'

She looked over into the parcel, and he looked round at us, smiling. She was one of those people whose legs look good without high heels. She bent down and picked up from the brown paper a black leather slipover, sleeveless.

'Try it on,' she said.

She went into Madeleine's room where there was a long mirror.

'It's good,' she said and came back in to us, looking beautiful and radiant because she enjoyed wearing different clothes.

'It's about the right size, too,' he said.

She was pleased to be reassured.

'You think you can get rid of some of these?' he said.

'I should think so. How much are they? That's the important thing.'

'Thirty bob,' he smiled and Simon and I looked at each other.

'Have a look at some of the other colours,' he said, yellow, brown, purple.

We joined her in looking. Simon liked the yellow and asked her to try it on as he reckoned his girl was about her size. The desire for something cheap, for a bargain, above all for something obviously with it, was infectious. I liked the brown. I wondered whether to fool myself it was for my sister.

'Ties, too,' he said, and thrust out a handful of suede ties.

'Ten bob, them,' he said. They were with it, too; he was wearing one himself, he pointed out.

Meanwhile she'd been examining the purple one and decided the lining which was in fact no lining but the reverse of the leather and so suede, was rather smooth too. It had got a flaw. Could they, she wondered, be reversible and flawless. There was the problem of the hemming.

'I'll have to see my contacts about that,' he said, and smiled. 'I couldn't say without checking on it.'

'It would be awfully nice if you could,' she said.

I examined myself in Madeleine's mirror in the brown one.

'You think you could get rid of some of them,' he said, obviously pleased at the response Simon and I had shown.

'I'm sure I could,' she said. 'I ought really to have a specimen, though, so they could see.'

They discussed this in a huddle. The idea seemed, on her part, to get one cheaper still for selling others. I wondered how she would find the time, with finals pressing, to sell leather slipovers, or where even she met this doubtful man. Simon pulled a face towards me, and I agreed; still, it was a chance, and I rather liked the brown one.

'Well, these are samples; I could let you have one tomorrow.'

'They won't be here,' she said, nodding at Simon and me.

We thought, and decided she could send them on to us. And then she went back to discussing the possibilities of reversible ones – double value for money – and the possession of a specimen, and the contacts. She was rather pleased, I think, to have shown us a little of her metropolitan life – and that we should take a souvenir of it back. It was certainly different from home.

When he'd gone we too had to go. I left her the thirty bob and she said she'd post it on when they got it, and I left her the possible postage money, remembering just in time. We wished each other luck in our various interviews, jobs, finals and lives. And grateful for the meal and above all for the peace and escape before the gruelling to come, we thanked her, awfully.

A large airliner, a Boeing 707, its undercarriage down, came in to land. I'd always been interested in aircraft and at home we weren't on any major civilian route. I watched it over the concrete skyline through the large fifth storey window of Broadcasting House, followed it round first with my eyes and then with my whole head.

'And what,' he said, his beetle brows heavy on a small and not pleasant face, frowning over his glasses, 'do you think of the present increase in crime?'

I'd never thought much about it.

'Well,' I said, and dragged my eyes back from the anyway disappearing Boeing, 'I suppose it is increasing.'

I didn't know, and tried to work out if it was; the personal touch rather than the abstraction of current affairs, that was the technique; and, of course, 'Oh, yes, I was, well just before I arrived,

I was in somebody's flat (and as she had done, for some reason I found it necessary to imply unequivocally the sex of the somebody) and I was waiting there before coming here.'

He was frowning at my twisting sentence which I threw out to give myself time to think.

'And some guy came in who was selling leather slipovers – you know, pullovers, only leather ones – for thirty bob. Well, I mean, it's obvious that for that money they must have been stolen. I suppose there is an increase in that sort of thing.'

I reflected, looking at the blank sky. But crime wasn't uniquely metropolitan, and I remembered with a surge of provincial patriotism, aggressive against the London which was closing in and bullying and constricting and asserting an unallowable superiority.

'And a friend of mine at home – well, someone I know, he's just been put on trial for knocking off a lorry load of tinned salmon.'

It wasn't strictly true, as it was the friend of a friend of mine, but I felt it necessary to assert that at home things happened, there were things to 'do' as well as in London, and I thought a modification for the personal touch, an assertion of the interest of my life too, legitimate.

He went on to ask me about the decline in importance of the family.

I took the parcel off the postman and ripped it open. It was rather a fetching piece of clothing and even if they didn't like it at home it would be different for a week or two at the jazz club and the county library. She'd put a brief note in, saying this was the thing, which was clear. She had felt, no doubt, that just to have sent a parcel would have been somehow wrong, insufficient; but she'd got nothing to communicate. As I didn't know Madeleine her problems and future were obviously not felt to concern me. 'Nice to see you,' she wrote. 'Do call in if ever you're up in London again. I do hope the interview went off all right and you get the job.'

The West Midland Underground

The West Midland Underground goes from   to . Or should I say went? Should I have said went? Should I be saying went? Or even will go. May go. Could go. Could have gone. Was to have gone. Is to go. Is to have gone. Is it possible to say is to have gone? Are there certain tenses that do not exist, may not, cannot, will not, did not; though now do? Perhaps the impossible tenses are needed for the impossible underground. Perhaps the hitherto impossible tense will bring into being the hitherto impossible West Midland Underground.

Henry James! Papua New Guinea has everything you could ever need. A brief example from a Papuan language of average complexity, Gadsup of the East New Guinea Highlands Phylum, may be given here to show the structure of the verbs occurring at the end of sentences – these are simpler verbal forms than the so-called medial forms. These sentence-final verb forms consist of a verb stem plus a number of elements suffixed to it. All these, linked together in a single long word, constitute the sentence-final verb forms, and such a verb form will show the following composition: verb stem + benefactor marker (that is, the action is carried out for the benefit of somebody) + potential marker +

ability marker + statement marker + interrogative marker + completion marker + subject marker + two emphasis markers (i.e. kùmù-ánk-àdád-òn-ték-áp-ón-i-nó-bé)… Thus the full shades of meaning of this elaborate verb form given above can be expressed in English only inadequately and may best be rendered by a sentence like 'had he indeed wanted to go down for him?'

Had she indeed wanted to go down for them? The nun. I recur remorselessly to the nun's tunnel. Like a movie of memory and compulsion, cutting back and back to those same frames. In the Gaumont, Worcester, I see *The Private Life of Sherlock Holmes* and *Underground*. *Underground* is about an officer parachuted behind German lines who works with the Maquis, shoots people, blows up bridges. Our truer underground runs still beneath. Sometimes buildings would collapse along the High Street, and we always believed they fell into the nun's tunnel.

> She trailed along behind the others as they returned along the underground corridor from the cathedral. At least having Mass there once a week was a change from the other six days when it was held in the nunnery. A change – but to what effect? She suddenly realized in all fullness how barren her life was, when she could call the difference between pious faces in the priory and the same pious faces in the cathedral a change.
>
> She jumped up suddenly. All the stored up misery had burst out, overwhelmed her. But she had sat there crying for too long. The door at the end of the passage would be closed, barred, bolted. She ran. She ran through the blackness of the corridor, on, on.

In 1959 I was writing about the nun's tunnel in the school magazine. In 1972 I add her into a story about cats in London. Why do I return to the nun's tunnel? The door was bolted. She died in the tunnel between the cathedral and the nunnery and her ghost still walks.

Was that the West Midland Underground? Does the West Midland Underground, alone of all undergrounds, have a ghost to parade along it? The White Lady of Worcester, patron saint of the underground. We could make a million, casting medallions of her for every freak's neck.

As for the dimensions, they are no more certain that the tenses.

Does the West Midland Underground		go historically,
Did	"	go topographically,
Will	"	go geographically,
May	"	go bibliographically,
Can	"	go chronologically,
Should	"	go adjectivally,
	from	
the Anglo-Saxons	to	the Industrial Revolution,
from the hills	"	the valleys,
from limestone	"	marl,
from Feckenham	"	Wyre Piddle,
from 1100 hrs	"	2300 hrs,
from bad	"	worse?

Where would we look for direction?

During the war the signposts were all taken down so parachuted spies wouldn't be able to find their way around. The land was without identity. When had the signposts first been put up, when had the land first been named for those who did not know the names? For those who grew from it, the names were always there, each land and hill, track and cluster of buildings. With merely an odd milestone for the aspirant Dick Whittingtons. And then came the century that broke the secrecies, that labelled the intimacies for anyone to see. The mysteries were revealed and the strangers spread over the land.

But with the war the labels and arrows were all erased; the surfaces were cleansed, and places existed only in themselves, their names accessible only for those who were at them, not for those who would only point. Perhaps it was then that the arrows to the W. Midland Underground were removed. And after the war, never re-erected. Perhaps they had got mislaid. Perhaps the men who pulled down the signs had died, or lost their memories, and nothing had been written down for fear the enemy might gain access to the records. So that there was nothing from which to rediscover the underground. Yet archaeologists could find traces of the old post holes if they looked. Though could they deduce the direction of the arrows from the post holes? The station entrances must lie there for discovery, beneath their thickets of brambles, their landslides of shale. Moles and ferrets and dormice scuttling into hiding there, bats hanging from the tunnel roofs to issue out at twilight.

Another possibility is that of deliberate closure by the overground; as with the canals. In my days of searching through the countryside I stalked the clues of this other possibility. I often crossed the canal, which canal it needs no more to answer than to question, exquisite brevity. And on the soft worn red brick bridges overarching the dried-up canal bed were rusted iron plaques, asserting ownership by the London and West Midland, or some such combination, steam locomotive company, taking us back to those days when the overground had bought the canal companies to close down their cheap competition. And could it be that the overground had bought out the underground, too, and affixed iron plaques of ownership to stations and arches and tunnels and platforms; and closed it down. And as the canals silted up and the lock gates rotted and crumbled and the reeds took over resuming the deep cut of the navvies back to the contours of the brambly hills, unseen, the tunnels collapsed behind their boarded entrances, the air chimneys piercing up through the hills were fenced off and bricked over and the briars and hawthorn spread across them, and within the bricks fell from the lining one by one, as tree roots and incautious moles pushed and encountered no resistance. The underground filled with the hollow bones of small animals and stale air; the heavy drapes of cobwebs closed off the passages that had fallen into disuse. While the overground roared above crushing the bed of granite chips beneath its steel tracks and creosoted sleepers.

RESEARCH SERVICE BIBLIOGRAPHIES / Series 4, no. 61 / Underground radio communication / Compiled by I. Boleszny / Adelaide / Public Library of South Australia / Australia / 1966.

At last our network of underground radio communication spreads the counter-culture through our global ether, underground nomadic transmitter caravans sending out new writing and revolution on accessible frequencies at the underground hours. What k/Ms will find them, what is the West Midland Underground transmitter's call signal? 'Articles prefixed by x are to the best of our knowledge not available in South Australia. Photocopies of these references can usually be obtained from libraries in other states and overseas. While this may sometimes be expensive, we have found that on most occasions the cost is about 2/- (20 cents) per page.'

1963.3. x Funktechnik unter Elektroakustik sowie
Sonderanlagen der Drahtnachrichtentechnik im Bergbau ...
H. Jahn. BERGBAUTECHNIK 13: 82–91, February 1963; 13: 131–45, March 1963.

4. New transducers for communicating by seismic waves. Il diag K. Ikrath and W. Schneider. ELECTRONICS 36: 51–5, April 12, 1963.

5. Investigation of the design of underground communication systems. L. M. Valles and others. IEEE TRANSACTIONS ON ANTENNAS AND PROPAGATION AP-11: 318–23, May 1963.

7. x. Electronic equipment for mine communications. R. E. Havener. MECHANIZATION 27: 52–4, March 1963.

8. Communications in mining industry. R. Lee. MINING JOURNAL 261: 30–3, July 12, 1963.

From about 3 a.m. there isn't much happening on the cab radio, we'll broadcast stories then. They'll be picked up by every cab operating. When the service gets known people will start taking cabs in order to hear the stories. Then we can extend to other times; eventually we'll broadcast twenty-four hours a day; we can have breaks for commercials, we can stop the story and give the cab calls, Bondi Road, Bondi to Darling Street, Balmain; Newcastle Hotel, George Street to St Vincent's Hospital; and then back to the story. We can even fit the messages into the story; we can have people phoning a cab in the story and we hear the operator calling the cab for them and when they're in the cab they listen idly to the cab radio calling 'Steyne Hotel, Manly to Sylvania Hotel,

Sylvania,' and so on, and they listen idly to the cab radio as long as there are messages to be transmitted; and if there aren't any messages to be transmitted they can be written into the story to create cab bookings. In the end the entire population of the city would be taking cabs in order to hear the stories. Different companies will run different programmes. It will be impossible to get a cab to travel in; people will be going into bookshops to buy short-story collections in order to travel home. 'Have you got the volume of stories *Seaforth Crescent, Seaforth to Mort Street*, Balmain?' 'This is the last one, sir.' 'Do I get a 10 per cent discount as a university teacher?' 'Not on paperbacks under a total of 23 miles, sir.' The biggest boom in the short story known to history will eventuate. The presses will be pouring volumes out, daily newspapers featuring them, special stories printed on cornflakes packages and Passiona bottles; fragments of stories: 'Collect the entire story from the ends of ten packets of meat pies.' New visitors to the city will have to discover the dead hour, in between the afternoon and evening story shifts; it will be as impossible to buy a short story between three and four p.m. as in the past it had been to travel by cab.

Gadsup was at college with me before he joined the East New Guinea Highlands Phylum. Even as an undergraduate, without the range of verbal forms that later was indeed to have become his, he had a knack of memorable expression. I remember one vacation entering The Cellars, a basement coffee lounge in which youth of the West Midlands gathered in their motor-cycling jackets and tattoos.

'I say,' he said as we sipped our coffee, his voice reverberating through the underground rooms, 'don't these marble-topped tables remind you of altars in a Greek temple? Diana at Ephesus or something?'

In the cellars the youth of the W. Midlands sat and looked.

'Just waiting for a human sacrifice.'

The coffee was very hot.

Likewise he once boomed out, entering a country pub, 'I'm thinking of writing a novel about someone who turns to Catholicism from excessive masturbation.'

The 'excessive' was a note characteristic of Gadsup, the shade of meaning he strode unerringly towards.

I wouldn't think the Salwarpe has trout. Don't trout streams have to be through limestone or something? Clear water? The Salwarpe wasn't clear; but ran slowly and muddily through clay, sandstone, trundled along. I use to canoe up it and that took about eight times as long as just walking because it meandered so much. It didn't really want to get to the Severn and lose its identity. So it kept winding from side to side. And didn't flow too fast. And then all the way along were these mills that had been there for centuries, damming up its hardly forceful flow, and letting what wasn't dammed up rush away through some narrow hurtling mill race, which as soon as it got round past the mill settled into the old comfortable sluggishness. Hawford Mill, Bill's Mill, Porter's Mill. Porter put up Queen Elizabeth when she went through, at one of his houses. I don't know who Bill was. But none of the mills works now; they just dam up water and the soft drink bottles and the twigs and the old boots, and let some of the other water hurtle down the mill race, which it probably likes doing, once in a while.

And then alongside the Salwarpe is the Wych canal, straight as a die. They ran together like two cops or two comedians, the straight one and the funny one, the nice one and the heavy one. There's a fable in it, too, sermons in stones and something in running brooks. Well, the canal isn't running any more. Back in the end of the eighteenth century it was Brindley's most beautiful canal, he said it was, and it ran as straight as a die from the Severn to Droitwich, to take the salt away. And all the way it ran straight the Salwarpe wriggled along beside it, making all these sinuous, concertinaed curves, like Marilyn Monroe alongside John Wayne. But there wasn't too much use for the straight canal and it silted up; there wasn't much use for the winding Salwarpe either; but it had always been there and had its own sources of water and current and so just kept on flowing not worrying any too much about use.

But just on the off-chance of trout I thought it might lead to the underground so I walked along, not exactly beside it since in that rainy winter everything had become pretty waterlogged, and between the old canal and the river, often a distance of only three or four yards or so, it tended to get a bit swampy; but I walked near it, along roads and paths that crossed over it or ran beside it and crossed back over it again. Till I came to this bare cleared patch of ground, and this high wire fence, and these new concrete buildings, and a label: Ladywood Pollution Control Unit. And down below the Ladywood Pollution Control Unit ran the Salwarpe. Maybe the West Midland Underground is a Dostoevskian underground.

The Salwarpe may have outlived John Wayne but technology gets its revenge in the end. Now they pour shit on the river I used to canoe along. And for certain there wouldn't be any trout there. And as the winter went on men with tractors and power saws went along the winding curling organic edge of the Salwarps and cut down all the willows that hung over it, all the hawthorn and elder and bramble that ran down from the bank to the water's edge; they cut away everything that might ever collapse and hold up the flow of shit into the Severn. They razed the edges of the Salwarpe flat like an airfield. Because if an old willow tree that had grown on the edge there for fishermen to sit under and kingfishers to fish under and mayflies to mill beneath, decided to lay itself down in the river that had undermined its roots all its years, decided just to surrender itself to the flow, then it would hold up all the shit, and they had to get the shit from the Ladywood Pollution Control Unit as quickly as ever possible into the Severn where it would be washed down with the fuller flow and eventually out to the Bristol Channel and America.

I guess the next they'll cut off all the corners of the old meandering Salwarpe which Brindley would've done if he could've done only he didn't have the technology but he thought of it, so the shit will just shoot down straight into the Severn without having to wind round at all; and then they'll concrete the whole top of the river over, with semi-circular pre-cast concrete culverts, and pump through double the volume; then they'll concrete over the Severn. Every river in the country will be arched over with pre-cast concrete culverts, arteries of shit being pumped along the old waterways, to form a solid, coagulate ring round the British Isles.

What are the advantages of looking for the West Midland Underground?

1. Health; daily walks through the clear air, good for the circulation, leg muscles, lungs, digestion.
2. Mental ease; the state of mental relaxation induced by walking through the country lanes, numbness.
3. Architectural; to explore the varieties of half-timbering, the black and white domestic architecture of the district. There is a barn built of stone, rare in this district, which a countryman who lives in the cruck cottage next to it said was stone left over from the church. That would be round about five hundred years ago. The corrugated iron roof was added later.
4. Historical; Warwick the Kingmaker was born in a half-timbered huge manor house beside the Salwarpe. On the skyline you can see Woodbury Hill where Caractacus made his famous last stand against the Roman invader.
5. Geographical; the way hills roll and rivers wind.
6. Botanical; flowers and plants and things, most of them not in flower yet. I can only tell their names when they're in flower.
7. Natural fauna; dormice, water rats, moles, but they stay underground and you can only see the mole hills; there are badgers underground too, I know where a badger set is, tunnelling into a ridge beside the old canal. Perhaps the fauna are there before us.
8. To talk to oneself watched only by cattle.
9. Fantasy. A long straight road, must be a Roman road running to Droitwich to get salt. Flat fields each side. Distantly, the clip clop of a horse. I walk, my breath white in the cold air. I am a dragon and behind a gentle knight is pricking on the plain. A lady with a headscarf,

riding jacket, jodhpurs; she turns to smile down on me. I turn to smile up to her, we wish each other good day. She rides on, along the straight road between the flat fields. She rides out of sight. At the crossroads I look for horseshoe marks in the mud at the roadside. There are horseshoe marks in all the mud, at every roadside, in every direction. For weeks I walk along the old Roman road, salt free, lady less.

10. Hope. Somewhere, over the rainbow, the crock of gold, the gates of Eden, the doors of bliss.

Coming to an End

So, there we were, for the last time again, looking at the menu which I don't think they had in the old days, I'm sure if there had been a menu I'd have written about it, about someone sitting there, fingering it, fiddling with it, turning it over and reading aloud from it, written that for something to begin with before getting going properly. We sat there down at the back, so we could see the whole length down to the glass front and open door, see people coming in and sitting sipping their coffees or cokes, and going out, and others coming. And three years ago, then it had been new; it had just been redecorated then, given a smooth sliding surface. They'd done that well; still it showed no marks of the time, no furrows of the years.

The waitress in black (and we remembered when they first put their waitresses into black),[1] Italian and sexual in a direct if middle-aged way, smiled with good teeth and went for our coffees.

'Well,' he said, and he said it with a sort of satisfaction.

'Well.'

'Three years and' – and drawing air in between his teeth – 'we're still here.'

And the mirror, which had seen us bored and pulling faces of Neanderthal man, an imbecilic chimpanzee, an old lady with no teeth, faces imitative of those we had just seen round us in the street and shops, the mirror reflected his sort of satisfaction. It proved a point.

Because getting away wasn't the same as being away; and coming back was very similar to never having moved. And three years of instruction in resigned paradox still didn't destroy the feeling when you came to it. The muzak tape played marches and songs of nautical patriotism, culminating in *Rule Britannia*, as if to reply to his Well with a gesture of equal, incontrovertible, defiant satisfaction. Never never never will be slaves.

And as three years before, and through the intermediate years, he unwrapped one lump of sugar and left the other, as all those times before, I took his unused sugar and chewed it, getting the same (in the way we would have written of it then, but now only with an apology) familiar kick from my teeth.

'Once,' he said, 'once it was something,' and a jerk of his head forward emphasized this something; to have come here.

New and unknown and probably wicked; we thought of other hell holes, the places of grim jest at the barmaid, the rumours and accounts of orgy. (!) It had been something because it was new and we were bored for the first time.

Harshly in the corner two Black Country suited men were chatting up the waitress; it was a study in phonetics. I said that to him; no thought was wasted. The waitress garnished her English with Italian, and the men grated unlovely sounds through the whine of factory sirens.

In the street the shoppers trotted by, and the office girls began to pass, and the faces, some the same and all familiar, came in and looked at the evening paper and drank tea and hoped. With its taped music and the coffee, with the image of the coffee bar and the waitresses there to serve your needs, it capitalized on the need for hope.

'I remember when coffee was fashionable', said my aunt. Phyllis Tweedcomely and I had some once; we were in York, and went into Ramskite and Knitworth's for tea.'

The coffee bar idea disseminated on TV made us all think something exciting might happen drinking coffee; and when I say all, I mean generously and presumptuously, my fellow men and women, my audience, good afternoon, and a very warm welcome to another edition of Auntie's Teatime. Now with us this afternoon to tell Phyllis Tweedcomely dirty jokes about the missionaries in Saudi Arabia is your friend and my friend –

The coffee bar idiom was an advantage in writing about the idea, about the young people in coffee bars. Autobiographically. It was simple, and having written it and shown it him, he used to agree it was all right; and it was, then.

> went by anyway. We just looked at the little waitress. She really was nice. I wish I could describe her. We couldn't look at her all the time, partly because she kept getting lost behind the Gaggia, partly because the old manageress bird was around. I don't know if she was the manageress. I don't know if they've even got a manageress. It was just that this old bird looked like one, which was bad enough. And we didn't want to spoil everything. So we had to be careful when we looked. Not that there was any point in it. I don't know really; sometimes I think Ken actually believes in it all. Life and that sort of thing. I'm pretty sure he was dead serious about the little waitress; I mean, he thought he could take her out. He hadn't the faintest clue how to go about it. How do you pick up waitresses? I mean if they sort of say no or scream or

Three years later we had been away and met new people and done new things if not had new experiences and learnt to write a little better. Differently, anyway. And while the coffee bar went on the same, for us it was now smaller and lesser, and yet in its minuteness getting larger and more oppressive because there was nothing much besides it. And going away, it's good to keep everything simple, make sure there are no involvements and make sure everything's wound up and concluded.

'You know the Birmingham road?'

'Si, yes.

'Well, theer's a pub up past the...'

We listened.

'You'll come?' the one asked.

'Si, I'll come,' she said, and smiled at them, and turned away from them at whom she'd been looking closely to understand their talk (oh to be a phonetician) the better.

There was a young waitress, leaning on the counter and looking across and I wanted to do as I had done before, to hammer on the table and say, 'I've been waiting twenty minutes' (and after all we had drunk our coffee nearly that time back), and then look at her and maybe she'd come over; but that was another story, and besides the wench is as good as dead. But it was the same country and the same town and the same coffee bar and the same, looking at the eyes, girl, basically. But leaving it's good to keep things simple; like we have always tried to do and usually so hopelessly succeeded in doing.

'It's just the same,' he said.

The coffee came; it was another waitress, not the one I liked. But she smiled so I smiled back. / 'I think my friend's taken a fancy to you,' she said. / Suddenly the bottom fell out of my stomach. I looked round. / 'Which?' I asked. I had to ask something. / 'Down there by the counter.' / The cute little one was standing by the Gaggia, looking towards us. I looked back and my mind somersaulted round and round. As it slowed down I leapt back on it and started to think. / 'What shall I tell her?' she asked. / 'I'm going away tomorrow,' I said. 'For a couple of months.'

I'd forgotten that episode, whose style I no longer liked, whose truth I doubted.[2] The one I was thinking of was intermediate, was sandwiched between these two ends, and I turned away from watching this young and lovely one looking across, and decided rather to wait for the coffee than start on another, to put it one way, story, that I might not care to write.

In fact the Italian brought us that second coffee as she had brought us the first, which would see us through until those God knows what hell holes[3] opened their arms, and we blotted out in beer, which was something we hadn't done so much three years back. And she went over to the two Black Country men, and they sat there, large, and suited in brown and blue, their buttocks flopping over the plastic and chromium seats, their backs broad and their necks thick and their hair oiled; and they smoked cigars, which were desecrating this place of our youth, into this temple of our first communion they brought the odour of money-lending and the taste of some success, they brought in the world that after three years, roughly, we ought to be going into.

'No,' he says, 'I want you, not your husband, I don't want to see him.'

And she showed those good teeth and smiled.

'But he will have to come as he drive the car.'

Through the front of the coffee bar, through the entrance where the glass door was held open against the wall, into the greying light of the street walked away the waitress who had looked, carrying her flat-heeled shoes in a plastic bag, and walking with slim legs and a shake of the head and a back held in the way it was just essential not to have seen, or to expunge from memory this time. And it was all wonderfully cinematic; which is as much as to say, it all existed, as it was, on its own terms, though there wasn't much else to it, and it wasn't to be reshaped and made into anything, since it was life, and the sort of life that couldn't be made into anything; And looking at it, cinematically (we sorted out this business of what, for us, then, cinematic meant, ten minutes or so later), looking at it he said,

'THE END.'

And I quipped splendidly,

'AN END.'

Because, like serials and so on, we had seen many endings and gone in the next time to see the whole cast there as before, the smudged make-up tidied for another try at the TV epic you will only see once:

THIS IS YOUR LIFE

And I remember years before all this started (this particular reel, that is; or should it be videotape?) saying to Alastair (who deserves a credit), 'I get worried lying in bed at night by an orchestra playing a piece of music which ends with say two or three drum beats; and then it doesn't end, but the drum beats again, an octave higher; and that isn't the end because it ends again with a tum-ti-tum rhythm; and then there's more to that, another drum beat, then cymbals – and it keeps on and on in my head and I just can't cut it off at an ending because another one keeps following, there never is a final ending.'

'What I do', said Alastair – and I doubt actually if this ever happened to him as he was different and things were different and the relation between things and him was different, but he would always give a solution – 'what I do,' he said, 'is pick up a revolver, and aim at the concert, and fire, and it all explodes and then everything's quiet.'

And even though I tried anti-tank guns it didn't end, because to kill them all the explosion had to be so great that bits kept falling down from the great distances to which they had been blown, bits one after another, all the time; and the explosion had done underground damage, and the earth kept caving in, suddenly, and separately, different areas, and long afterwards when the stray cats roaming thought everything was over and peaceful, they dislodged a stone to precipitate some further collapse, and then bits of loose plaster would slowly drop.

Walking out through that place we had left so many times, and heading for the bus stop, we saw a shop window with a large poster announcing the Nirvana or the Paradise of the Seventh Heaven Coffee Bar.

OPENING SHORTLY

And he turned to me and said, with a wonderful concluding line, as his bus came in, his last words, 'Well, that's one place we shan't be going in, thank God.'

I remember at school Alastair and Gordon and I, after Gordon had said Oscar Wilde had shown no signs at all when he was our age then, agreeing to meet in ten years time (though we never have done), to check up on how we had developed, to have a sort of reunion and reassurance.

And not arranging a reunion was no reassurance that three years hence, as three years before, it wouldn't all come round again to the same thing.

As his bus moved out I shouted, 'Saturday night, seven.'
'For the last time,' he said, 'seven.'
I'm going to open an all-night coffee bar called Hell.

Coda

When I got to Sydney there was already one called the Inferno.[4]

Notes

[1] 1960
[2] I'm sure now that it was the one I liked who brought the message, and the one I didn't like who had taken the fancy.
[3] (!)
[4] But it closed three years later.